Lock Down Publications and Ca$h
Presents

I0637475

THE MURDER

QUEENS 6

A Few Minutes 2 Late

Written By
Michael Gallon
and Rhynyia (Sexy Redd) Santiago

First Edition 2024

Printed in the United States of America

Lock Down Publications
P.O. Box 944
Stockbridge, GA 30281
www.lockdownpublications.com

Like our page on Facebook: Lock Down Publications
www.facebook.com/lockdownpublications.ldp

Stay Connected with Us!

Text **LOCKDOWN** to 22828 to stay up-to-date with new releases, sneak peaks, contests and more…

Like our page on Facebook:
Lock Down Publications

Join Lock Down Publications/The New Era Reading Group

Visit our website:
www.lockdownpublications.com

Follow us on Instagram:
Lock Down Publications

Email Us: We want to hear from you!

Prologue

Early Thursday morning, the time now had to be around 7AM. I had no idea as to the time, since the Lakeland Police Department still had me sitting inside one of my dining room chairs, ducked off inside my laundry room. After me and one of the cops had got into a bit of a scuffle, my head and mind were still a drift. All I could think of was what had happened to cause them and Homeland Security to be at my condo so early on a day like this?

That was a good, dire question and the answer to that must be for me taking my girlfriend, Honey, on the previous night to purchase a dub sack of weed. But instead of them asking me questions about the weed and who I bought it from, they were asking me questions about the group of females I had called the Florida Hot Girls. Not one damn time did they reference them to that name. Instead, they continued to deem me as a fucking pimp. A word that I had told many people during the course of my tenure as their manager and owner that I wasn't.

Then, the other question was where was my gotdamn girlfriend, Honey? Man, Honey was exactly like her stage name. *Honey*. She was beautiful, or more like gorgeous. From the first moment I laid eyes on her, I knew that I had to have her. Even though I already had a few females on my list of women that I called my own. Like this one cute lil red bone from Lake City, Florida. Her name was Jessica. Fine lil thang with light green eyes. But to me, Honey was who I wanted and desired to be with. So, as I sat there inside of that chair, in that small, cramped room, I thought of her and what were they doing to her fine ass.

Little did I know, they had her ass at McDonald's buying her ass breakfast. And me, seated inside a chair with my damn stomach touching my ribs. I was so fucking hungry that all I could think about was back to that day, where my brother and I were down on a small island outside of Puerto Rico. That exact place, I have to keep secret. All due to what you are about to read, right about now... This is the continued Saga of The Murder Queens!

Chapter 1
The Amvets

It was a hot, sunny day, balmy if you ask me. Not too hot nor too low in temperature. In other words, just right for a brother like myself. My brother and myself along with my queen were on the small island that her and her family called home. Before we all arrived on her father's private jet plane, she made me and my brother promise to never tell a soul about his hidden paradise. I assured her I wouldn't, but as far as my dumb witted brother was concerned, I couldn't vouch for him. Hell, she had even asked me to not do any business with her very powerful father. I gave her my word that I wouldn't and to this day, I have never crossed that line. But James "Smooth" Valentino Junior, would.

In the end, the line that he crossed would cause many people to lose their precious life over. All for just the chance to partake in the white powdered substance her father, Pierre Santiago sold. The enticing drug was so powerful that it would leave many people craving it, more than the air that we breathe. In the end, it would bring my brother to his knees, right before Pierre Santiago cut his head completely …

The island was a beautiful sight to see, and I enjoyed every bit of our short lived stay. We had planned on staying for about two weeks. You know, attend her brother's funeral and then enjoy a much-needed vacation away from the hustle and bustle I was accustomed to. But as you will see, my foolish brother had other plans for me and him. Now at this present time, while I sit back in this cell that the government has confined me to, I can reflect back to that very day that all of our lives would be changed forever. I remember it just like yesterday, when we were with her and her prestigious family.

Rhynyia had just introduced us to her Uncle Felix and you could get the uncanny sense of his influence within their intriguing family. She held the utmost respect for her uncle as she claimed that if not for him, she would have never known how to fire a weapon. For it was him who took the time out of his busy schedule to show her how to aim and fire a weapon. I guess that you can say he was the one who taught his lil precious niece how to kill. A skill set that she had learned to master by the tender age of ten. By fifteen, she was a professional at what she did best.

By the age of twenty-five, she had fully mastered what he had instilled inside her. My brother and I sat there observing and listening to how the both of them interacted with one another. That was until he called out to one of the waiters.

"Hey Pablo, come here please?"

He quickly arrived with a bright smile on his face. "Yes sir, what can I get you?" Pablo asked, his warm smile never leaving his face.

"Take their orders for me."

"Yes, senor," he uttered and then took Rhynyia's order first.

Meanwhile, her uncle looked from me to my brother and asked. "So which one of you is it that has swept my gorgeous niece off of her feet?"

'Damn, he couldn't see and realize that by looking at the both of us?' I said to myself as I placed a side smirk on my face and stared over at my country looking ass brother, who hadn't been outside Madison, Florida, until this day and time.

Rhynyia had placed her order, then placed her right hand on her uncle's left hand and said. "Uncle Felix, may I introduce to you, Michael Vallentino, my fiancé and his brother, James Lorenzo Vallentino Junior."

Just as she finished, I stood to my feet and shook his hand.

"Fiancé?" He remarked as he paused. "So when did this happen? I thought that you and him were only a couple, who dated one another?"

"It's nice to meet you, sir. And we were, but I proposed to her just before takeoff, while we were back in Orlando," I replied as Rhynyia flashed her engagement ring in his face. He slowly took her hand and pulled her finger closer to stare at the huge diamond ring that sat so nicely on her ring finger.

"Wow, I must admit that the young man has great taste. Let's just hope that my brother is accepting when it comes to this ring. And his proposal of you becoming his wife," he said to us as our food arrived back at the table.

"Umph, I guess he told you, huh, baby brother?" Smooth remarked as he gulped down his drink.

"Whatever, my nigga," I quickly interjected as kept my side smirk on my face.

"Oh, he shouldn't have any problems, if so, I'm sure that he will get over them," Rhynyia spoke up for me and the ring as we dug into our nice looking food.

"Well with that said, let's all dig into this good-looking food before it gets cold," her uncle uttered.

While seated there eating, her uncle looked over at me and asked me the million dollar question. "So, what part of Florida are you from Michael?"

Without hesitation I answered back with. "I'm originally from a small town by the name of Madison, Florida. My parents moved when I was two to a small city called Lakeland, Florida. But now, I reside in Orlando, Florida," I said all of this while looking him directly in his eyes, showing him that I wasn't intimidated by his wealth and fame.

He then shook his head in approval as he came back at me with. "Ahh, beautiful Orlando, Florida. It's a very nice place to visit. That's where my brother met Rhynyia's mother," he said as he looked up into the sky, like he was searching for answers that she was about to ask him.

With a radiant smile on her face, she dropped her fork and said. "So, Uncle Felix, do you know what part of Orlando it was where my father met my mother? I looked for her while I was there, but I could never find her."

Then just like if he had just been in Orlando yesterday, he came back with. "Yes, I can remember it as if it was yesterday. We were at this one club called The Amvets and there was this young attractive looking lady who was there with her friends and sisters. They must have just turned the right age to enter and couldn't get into the club. I remember because your persistent father helped them get into the club that night." He paused to take a sip of his beverage, then continued with. "Your beautiful mother was starstruck by your father, who pursued her heavily all that night. After a few weeks of them conversing with one another, she agreed to meet your father for dinner. Well one thing led to another and before we knew it, she became pregnant with you."

Her eyes grew larger as her uncle continued. "My brother continued dating her until one day her father found out that the father of her baby was of Hispanic descent. Plus, your dearly departed grandfather investigated my brother and our family history. Once he found out who we are and what we stand behind, he was outraged. So outraged that he demanded that she stop seeing him. Your mother was heartbroken by her father's decision."

Hot tears began to well up in her eyes as she stared at her uncle. Becoming a bit choked up, she said. "Please tell me more. What happened next?"

"Well, after you were born, your father vowed to never keep you away from his side. He tried to bring you and her here with us to this very same island. But your grandfather stopped you and your mother at the airport. Your mother agreed to let you come back to Puerto Rico, with your father, only if you were allowed to come visit her from time to time.

"So, why don't I remember her or any of the visits?" She asked with her hot tears cascading down her face.

I was so shaken up with the story, I had to place my hand over her hand to let her know that I was there for her.

"It seems as though after a few years of you traveling back and forth, they both lost contact with one another. Causing you to be raised here in Puerto Rico. You were really too young to remember her," he said as a few tears of his own escaped his eyes.

While he wiped away at one of his tears, she said something that startled everyone at the small quaint table. "You know Uncle Felix, I keep having this same terrible nightmare of being in a car with a beautiful woman and older gentleman and in the dream, the car crashes and I'm whisked away by some men with their faces covered."

"What else do you remember about this dream?" He asked, now face holding onto a sinister glare. "All I know is that when I was taken from the accident, I could faintly remember one of the men saying to me. "It's alright my child, your safe now."

"Have you ever told anyone of this terrible nightmare?" He asked, still looking sinister.

"Not really, I guess because it's a dream, but it keeps coming back to me. By the way, whatever happened to my grandfather on my mother's side?"

"I have no idea. All I know is that he died some time ago." he replied as from out the corner of my eye, I could see what looked like a very bad scar on his neck, with a few burns on his hand.

"Excuse me Uncle Felix, where did you acquire the scar and burned hand from?"

He looked surprised by the question and quickly answered with. "From a terrible accident as a small child."

'Yeah right!' I thought to myself as he still looked a bit suspicious …

Chapter 2
Choked Half to Death

As I sat there studying her Uncle Felix, I could get the daunting feeling that he wasn't being completely honest about his scars. Even Rhynyia cut her eyes over at me, with a bit of her own skepticism. I guess she realized that we had her uncle up against the ropes, because she came back at him with another question, that actually would cause my black ass to choke half to death.

"So Uncle Felix, do you remember my mother's name? Or where I might start to search for her at?"

"Yes, I think that her name was *Karen* or *Carol* or something like that," he spoke as I dropped my gotdamn fork into my plate of curry chicken and begin to cough, violently at the mention of that name.

I guess it must have caught my country ass brother off guard as he immediately began patting on my back, rashly asking me. "Bruh, you alright, what's wrong?"

Apparently I was choking on the food that I was trying to consume, you idiot! I said to myself as I turned towards him, trying to tell his ass to stop hitting me in my damn back so damn hard.

Seconds turned to minutes as I nonchalantly looked over at Rhynyia while putting my hands over my mouth, desperately trying to cough up whatever it was that was causing me to choke. "Get him some water, just don't let the man choke to death."

By me being so agile and quick on my feet, quickly thinking before I choked half to death, I reached out for the glass of white wine that was sitting in front of me. Once I had my glass in hand, I quickly drank it, before my life was over. After choking for about three minutes, I gained my composure as her uncle looked over at me and asked. "Are you okay, my friend?"

"Yes, I'm good now. Thanks for asking."

"No problem, I would hate it if you would have died here inside of my restaurant. All because of a piece of chicken."

"Yeah, me too," I replied as a gentle smile beamed across my face.

"Bae, are you sure that your good? Or do we need to get you some medical attention?" Rhynyia asked as she had a worried look on her face.

"No, I'm quite alright, baby girl," I uttered as her uncle turned back towards Rhynyia and muttered. "You know what, come to think about it Rhynyia, I may have a picture of your gorgeous looking mother inside of my office. It's tucked away in one of my files."

She swiftly placed her hand on her uncle's hand and uttered. "It would be so helpful to me if you could find that picture of her for me."

Without any hesitation he quickly said. "Hold on one minute, beautiful, let me go see if I can find it for you."

Her Uncle Felix swiftly stood to his feet, and dashed off towards his office, in search of the dubious picture that would enlighten one world, while shattering another.

"I really hope that he still has that picture, Michael."

I was stuck right there, left with nothing to say. I was so caught up with what if he found that picture? Then she would definitely know who her mother was.

"Michael, do you hear me talking to you?" She asked as she snapped me back to reality. This is when I picked up my glass of wine and slowly sipped, then replied.

"Yeah, me too Rhynyia, me too. But why would he have a picture of your mother instead of your father, Rhynyia?" She stared at me with a quizzical look on her face as she replied. "I don't have the slightest idea,. All I know is that I would love to see a more up to date picture of her. Then, you can go back to Orlando and search for her before I return," she said.

"Yes, that would be nice. But how could he have an up-to-date picture? It has to be some years ago when he seen her last. If he did have an up-to-date picture, it would mean only one thing," I uttered.

It didn't take her long to come up with an answer as she quickly restored. "Your absolutely right, that would mean one thing," she mumbled as dumb witted Firstborn stopped chewing and asked.

"What's that, sis?"

She looked at me, then back at him with one answer. "It means that he must be in some type of contact with her."

"Damn," he uttered as he gulped down the rest of his wine, then holding up his glass, trying to get the waiter's attention. As he did that, she excused herself from the table with. "Bae, excuse me while I go and try to help him find that picture."

Quickly standing to my feet I uttered. "Go right ahead, bae, you do that."

She then fleetly walked away, with her four henchmen in tow.

"So are you okay now, lil bruh?" My brother asked me as I sat back down.

"Yes, but I get this feeling I just might know who her mother is already?"

"What?"

"Yeah bruh, and the answer I give you is going to knock your fucking socks off."

He quickly looked down at his feet. Then, bringing his head back up. "Bruh, I don't have any socks on."

"Nigga, it's just a saying." I shot back with my lips curled up.

"Oh, my bad."

I quickly fell back hard up against my chair as I shyly picked up my near empty glass, then coyly looking back over at Firstborn. "You're not going to believe who in the hell her mother is!"

He stopped chewing and drinking as he stared into my face with those big ass eyes of his and asked. "Who?" ...

***

Back in beautiful Orlando, Florida. Over at the hospital, Ms. Sharon Conoly had just been painfully placed in her temporary wheelchair, when the nurse bent over and said. "Okay ma'am, could you please sign these release papers so that we can get you on your way?" She grimaced in dire pain as she reached for the clipboard and signed her name, then holding out her hand for her bottle of pain medication.

Minutes later, her mother impatiently wheeled her cute ass out to her car, trying to get them out of the blistering, hot Florida sun. Bre was sitting in her mother's lap, smiling back at her mother.

"Why are you smiling so hard at me, lil girl?" Sharon asked her daughter, while trying to paint a smile on her face. "Because my mommy is coming home with me," the cheerful young girl muttered as Sharon's mother wheeled the both of them out of the hospital.

Now with her daughter in her arms, she felt as though her life had a new beginning to it, since she had disposed of the man responsible for kidnapping her and her daughter. She hadn't heard anything as to how Lt. Richards was doing and frankly didn't give a fuck. Just as long as her and her family were safe and still alive. All she could do now was to pray and hope that her problems were finally over and behind her, so as she uncomfortably, sorely sat inside of her mother's car, she happened to glance over at her and said a silent prayer to Yahweh; for allowing her and her daughter to escape from her horrid ordeal.

After opening up her eyes, she cut a glance over at her mother, Karen and said. "Hey mom, something has been puzzling me ever since I came too."

"What's that, honey?" Her mother asked as she tried to maneuver out of the crowded parking lot.

"That girl."

"What girl, Sharon?" Her mother asked, cutting her eyes in her direction. "The girl that I was trying to tell you about, before I dozed off. The one who's lap I was in when Michael and his crew of women rescued me and Bree."

The constant thought of the woman's face kept playing throughout her head as she sat there trying to enjoy her ride back to her humble abode.

While her mother drove through traffic, she tried to keep her eyes on the road and her daughter, when she looked back over at her and said. "Is it that important to you Sharon, that you know who the faces belong too?"

"Yes, mother, for some odd and very strange reason I know that I've seen that girl's face somewhere before. I just can't seem to put my finger on it right now."

"I'm sure it was one of the girls that worked with your man, Michael." Then as if she was hit over the head with a ton of bricks, Sharon quickly blurted out. "That's exactly where I remember seeing her face at now! She was the girl in the picture!"

"What damn picture, Sharon?" Her mother asked as she made a screeching stop at the red light, causing smoke to smell from the burnt rubber. "The damn picture that those detectives showed me the day they came by the house asking questions about the disappearance of Uncle Fats!" Sharon uttered as she stared at the face of her mother, who held some secrets of her own, that she prayed that they stayed right there.

"Wait a minute, so you're trying to tell me that the female who was last seen with my baby brother, was the female who was with Michael the night they rescued you and Breanna?" Karen then tried to remember the few faces that she had seen with me, the night at the hospital after rescuing Sharon and Bre.

Sharon made sure that Bre was seated in her car seat properly, before saying. "Yes, I'm positive that the girl in the picture is the same damn girl!" She said with adrenaline pumping through her heart.

"Sharon, wait a minute before you start jumping to conclusions. Think about it, that would only mean one thing." She paused as she looked deep into her daughter's eyes.

"I already know, ma.," Sharon said with conviction.

"Then, Mr. Michael knows way more than he's telling us. You don't think that he had something to do with his disappearance, do you?"

She turned her head from her mother, staring out of the window. She then slowly turned to look back at Karen and said. "I don't know, mom and I would sure as hell hate to find out that he did. Because if he had something to do with that, there's no telling what else his sneaky ass is up to or capable of doing."

Then, Karen uttered something that might just cripple my love affair with her daughter. "You're right. Not only that my dear Sharon, but what if him and those women of the night that he has, running around with him all day, had something to do with the murder of Do Dirty and her friends?"

***

Entyce and the girls had been back home for several hours after they tied up their loose strings over in Daytona. She was just walking out of her bathroom when her boyfriend,

Reese turned over in bed and asked her. "So, what show did you all have last night?"

"Why do you ask, bae?" She replied, not really feeling like being questioned about what she did in order to support him and her.

"Because, the last time I checked, you guys had lost the spot over at the Caribbean Night Club," he stated as he sat up in bed. The same bed that was at the house his sorry ass was living in.

"Okay, well maybe we had something else to do," she answered with a bit of sarcasm laced in her mild mannered voice.

"Yeah, like what?" He asked, now standing to his feet. He might not have wanted to poke the bear though. Something he was definitely about to find out.

"Listen, when your lil short stanking ass starts paying rent round this muthafucka, then and only then can you ask me questions about what it is that I do with my off time!" She angrily replied.

"Hold on, you don't have to talk to me that way! Remember, it was you who asked me to come stay with yo' ass!" He barked as he stood there with nothing on but a pair of white boxers.

Entyce stopped at the door of the room and then turned back towards him with fire in her eyes. "And that was because your broke ass didn't have a place to stay. Now if you have somewhere else that you can live, please leave. Matter of fact, leave any fucking way. I don't need no broke ass, ex wanna-be 69 Boyz dancer, living off of my ass anyway!" She was livid. Even more livid when she thought back to when he first came to live with us. There was one occasion where after a night at one of the clubs we danced at. Some guy wanted a night along with Entyce, all to himself. He even wanted to pay her a cool thousand dollars for that one night of pleasure.

Well when the guy looked over her body and told her his price, she kindly looked back at the guy, then over at her new boyfriend and said. "I'm sorry bae, I'm with my man and I'm pretty sure he wouldn't want me to be out selling my body for cash." Reese heard the amount the man wanted to pay and crushed her ass with. "Girl, you better go get that money!" We all knew what type of relationship he wanted after that night.

Now as he stood there in his body with what Entyce had just told him, he tried to look sad as he came back with. "So, that's how you feel?"

"Yep and if you need any help packing what clothes that I paid for, ask the help to help your broke ass pack!" The door of the bedroom shook the entire house as she angrily slammed the door, then walked downstairs. She stormed right past Mignon, who was walking back upstairs, when she stopped her dead in her tracks.

"Hey, you okay?" Entyce stared back at her before saying. "Yeah, just pissed off with his lil nosy, short ass!"

"Why, what did he do now?" Mignon asked as she chewed on a handful of raisins.

"The nigga is getting too damn nosy for me. Asking me where we were last night, since we lost the Caribbean!" She replied as a bit of saliva sprayed across Mignon's face.

Mignon propped her ass up against the rail of the stairs and then muttered, while wiping off the spray of saliva. "Yeah, I can see where you're going with this. It's probably best that his ass leaves anyway. Before we have to put a hole in his ass for tipping off the cops about what it is that we do."

Chapter 3
Santiago!

It was getting late in the evening, as we say down in Florida. And hot ass Lil Kitty was growing impatient by the minute since Richard hadn't called her back with the information she desired. So she took it upon herself to place the call. Mignon was still talking with Entyce, when she felt her phone vibrating up against her sensual looking hips.

"Hold on girl, let me get this," she said as she frowned at the name the caller ID displayed the name of Hot Booty ass Lil Kitty.

"Who is it?" Entyce asked as she seen the displeased look Mignon had.

"Nobody girl, just hot ass Lil Kitty," she uttered as both of them laughed. "Hello."

"Hey Mignon, sorry to bother you, but did Richard call you yesterday about this weekend?"

"Yes he did, girl, why? What's up?" Mignon asked, really not desiring to speak with Lil Kitty.

"So what up, are we going to Jacksonville this weekend or what?" Lil Kitty asked.

"Why Lil Kitty?" She asked, lips curled up and a very disgusted look on her face.

"Because it's some niggas up there who won't to spend that bread with us this weekend. That's why?" She said as she violently began coughing out some of the weed smoke that she could contain in her small ass lungs.

"I don't know right now. You know how Mike is not here and all. And he really hates for us to travel that far out of town without him," Mignon versed as she rolled her eyes inside her head.

"Maaan! Forget about Mike. His black ass is out having fun for the week, when we all need to make our bread back here," she spat as she took another long pull from the weed.

"I hear you, Lil Kitty. Tell you what, let me think about it for a few more hours. When I have an answer, you will be the first to know."

Lil Kitty sighed after a deep breath, then spoke back with. "C'mon Mignon, let's just go. These dudes even claim that they will pay for our rooms if we all come up there."

Mignon began to shake her head from side to side as she glared over at Entyce. "Hold on for one minute," Mignon said as she placed the phone to her hips.

"Yeah," Lil Kitty replied while she held on.

Mignon then asked Entyce. "So, what do you think? Should we ride up or what?"

"Might as well, do we have any other shows planned for the weekend?"

"Not as I know of, but you know how things change so fast round here."

"Well, looks like we all head up to Duval for the weekend," Entyce muttered.

"Cool," Mignon replied, then held the phone back to her ear and said. "Okay Lil Kitty, call your people and let them know that it's on for the weekend. Who are these clowns anyway?" She asked as she placed her phone on speaker.

"You don't know him, but his name in Punkin," Lil Kitty answered with a wide ass smirk on her face.

Just as soon as Mignon heard his name, she knew something might be off. "That's the nigga that was with them jits who fucked Strawberry over that morning. Matter of fact, they sent her ass back with a wet ass and no fucking money!"

Mignon shouted out. "Oh shit, you're right, Mignon." Entyce chimed in with.

"I don't know about all of that, all I know is that they really want to see us," Lil Kitty spat back, hoping that Mignon didn't change her mind.

"Yeah, alright, Lil Kitty, we'll see you on Friday. Peace." Mignon then hung up her phone, staring at Entyce. The both of them were frozen in time as they looked at one another.

"You know what that sounds like, right? A straight set up!" They both looked up at the top of the stairs, staring at Strawberry.

"Your right, Strawberry, so you know what that means?"

"Yep, we have to get our shit together. Because it seems like another very long weekend," Strawberry uttered as she walked down stairs, with neither of the women even knowing that somebody was ear hustling on their entire conversation through their bedroom door…

***

As Sharon and her mother rode home, the mere thought of Michael knowing more than what he was saying, had them both sitting there, mentally drifting from one scenario to the other one. They tried to change the subject, but their conversation would only resort back to the dreadful thought of what if. Things didn't change when Sharon looked over to her mother and asked her.

"So has the police had any luck with finding your brother?"

"If they have, they haven't contacted us," Karen replied.

"Damn, poor Uncle Bernard. I hope and pray that he's somewhere safe and sound," Sharon uttered, face staring out of the passenger window. "Me too, Sharon, me too."

"Me too, mommy." Breanna shouted from the backseat.

Sharon turned around and cut a half smile at her daughter, then turning back around placing her hand on her mother's hand. "Michael has a lot of questions to answer when I see him."

"When is he due back in town anyway?" Karen asked, face facing forward, making sure she drove through traffic.

"I don't know. He went to attend a funeral."

"Where?" Head on a swivel as she looked at Sharon, then back at the road up ahead.

"Somewhere over in Puerto Rico," Sharon uttered as she looked up ahead also.

"Puerto Rico, huh?" Karen probed as she felt a lump form in her throat.

"Yes ma'am."

"Now who does his ass know over there?" Karen asked, not ready for what her daughter was about to say. "Some family by the last name of Santiago."

"Who?" Karen asked as she damn near ran off of the road at the mere mention of the last name, Santiago!

Chapter 4
Bye Punkin

Karen swiftly gained her composure and control of her car, without causing any harm to any of her precious cargo. Her actions did cause her head to swirl back and forth as if it was on a swivel. Then, she modestly looked over at Sharon, then to the backseat, making sure that Breanna was okay.

Sharon was just as shocked as her mother was as she looked over at her and asked. "What's wrong, are you okay, or do you need me to drive us home?"

At first she had to take a deep breath, then she replied back with. "I'm so sorry baby, something darted out in front of the car," she lied as she swerved back into traffic, maintaining her path of travel.

"What, because I never saw anything?" Sharon wittily remarks, while turning her head to make sure Breanna was still safe in her car seat. "Seriously, something ran out in front of me. Now go on, what were you saying about the family he was going to visit over in Puerto Rico?"

Sharon had just turned her head back around to the front, still shaken up as she uttered. "All I know is that it has something to do with the one chick that he sees from time to time."

"So, you're telling me that Michael is dating you and someone else?" Her mother asked with a puzzled look on her face.

"Something like that. All I know is when he gets back. I'm telling him that it's either me or her, because I really can't deal with him not being here with me. Especially with me being pregnant with his child and all."

"I'm surprised that you're with him now." Karen tried to put her two cents in. "What's the name of the female he's seeing over in Puerto Rico?" She then asked, secretly preparing herself for the answer, that she didn't want to hear.

"Like I said before, mom before you damn near killed me and Bre. The family's last name is Santiago."

"From where?" Her mother asked, as if she just had to know more.

"Well, the girl used to live here in Orlando, but had to go back to Puerto Rico, to help bury a family member. I can't remember her first name, but I think it starts with R or something like that." Her mother knew what her name was, but couldn't show any signs of her knowing, but she had to know. The pressure was causing her to have hot flashes all over her body. "How don't you know her name and she's dating your man?"

"Damn ma, you really act like you must know. What, are you dating Michael too?" Sharon asked out of frustration.

"No child, I'm just asking, that's all," she said in her defense. "I only met the chick one time and that was at the club when I caught his ass with her. Come to think about it, me and this bitch, almost look like we could be sisters."

That was when Karen shouted back at her with. "What? You're kidding right? How does she look for real, Sharon?"

"Damn ma, you act as if you want to meet her or something?"

Karen was caught off guard by that comment, as she cunningly averted with. "It's not that, honey. I was just curious, that's all."

"You sure? Because your asking questions like you want to get to know the girl, just as bad as I do!" Sharon versed as she stared at her mother.

"I'm sorry, if it seemed that way, please forgive me. I tell you what, let's just change the subject.

"Yes, please," Sharon said, then blurted out. "And I think the chick's name is …"

"Mommy, I have to use the bathroom!" Bre shouted from the backseat, cutting Sharon off in mid-sentence and stopping her from telling Karen what she desired to know…

***

Lil Kitty was thrilled to death about the good news. Now all she had to do was to call her Lil Boo Thang and let him know of what was going on. Punkin's phone rang two times as he turned down the music that was beating inside of his all black box Chevy Caprice. His narrow ass lips turned sideways as he saw who it was calling.

"Hey you, been waiting on your call all day," he lied as he placed his arm up against the driver side window of his car, stopped at the red light.

"Yeah, I bet. Whatever, whatcha doing?" Lil Kitty asked as she walked inside of the apartment she shared with her grandmother and small son.

"Nothing, just cruising through Duval, thinking bout cha," he replied, slight smirk on his face.

"Whatever." She quickly spat back.

"For real, lil ma."

"Okay, I'm going to see just how much you were thinking about me."

"Oh, so what, y'all making the trip this weekend for sho?"

"Hell yeah, I just got off da phone with ole girl. So everything is a go."

"Dat's what's up," he said as he kept right on smirking. "How many rooms do I need to get for y'all?"

"Hell, with all da bitches dat's in dis group, I'm gonna say at least five or six of them thangs," she spat back. Lil Kitty was real ghetto. She was raised in the ghetto and talked just like a hood chick, but with a cute face and banging lil petite body. Deep down inside of me, these some years later, I will be the first to admit, Lil Kitty was my secret lil boo thang that I still hold a special place in my heart for. But truth be told, I believe all of those females who started the Florida Hot Girls with me, will always have that special place in my heart. I say that, because every single one of them were always 100. They kept their appearance and mouth tight. Now shaking my head, if only a few of them bitches from Lakeland, Florida would have done the same, I probably wouldn't be where I am now. But because of them, you all get to read the entire true story.

Now where did I leave off? Right after she told Punkin the news about them making that dreadful trip, he came back at her with. "Okay, well I'm going to grab at least eight rooms, just to be on the safe side."

"Damn, you caked up like that?" She asked, mind already thinking about all the money she was going to make that weekend. But the only person that was going to get her money was the got damn weed man. "Something like that, Lil Kitty."

"I really don't care how many of them you get, just make sure that you have one especially for me and you. Because I'm going to put my lil clit all over them thin ass lips of yours."

That really brought a full smile on his face as he gave the high-powered machine some gas and sped through the traffic light. "Dat's what I like to hear, I can't wait. So y'all will be here on Friday, round what time?" His impatient ass asked.

"I really don't know, but we like to always get in whatever town we are doing a show at, early, so we can all go shopping before the show. So I say at least before five or six that evening.

"Sounds good to me, I'll holla at cha later, peace," he said as he hung up his phone, ready to call his partner and relay the good news.

"Bye Punkin," she uttered, not even knowing of the danger she had just placed the girls in. Leaving me and my brother in the blind as to what was about to take place. It was the one most important thing I always told those females.

"Never give your phone number out!" Something that was forbidden while being a member of my elite group of women. But some years later, one of my females from Lakeland, Florida, by the name of Trina gave her number to a guy we had a show for in some small town in Georgia. Well as you guessed it, he called her when we arrived back home. Told her that his mother had died and wanted her to come to the funeral with him for support. She did. He needed some support alright. After the funeral, his aunt died, and she stayed another week. But after that, he kidnapped her and held her ass until a few of the Murder Queens went and rescued her lil naive ass …

***

As her mother pulled into Sharon's driveway, the first thing she witnessed was her car. She was thrilled that it had been returned to her house just as she had left it the day Lt. Richards and his crooked ass partner, John Hatfield had pulled her over and kidnapped her. What a relief it was for her since she thought that she would have to go down to the police pound to retrieve it.

"Boy, am I glad to finally be back home," she said as she eased out of the passenger seat.

"I hear you. I'm thankful your here too," Karen replied, mental still pondering if her long lost daughter was the female I was seeing.

Sharon was glad to finally be back in her humble abode, in her own comfort zone. A place she thought that she would never see again. Just as she got to the front door and placed her key inside, she had to utter. "Thank you Yahweh." She then opened up her eyes and placed her house key into the door of her home.

"What was that, Sharon?" Her mother asked.

"Nothing ma, just thanking the man up above, that's all," she said as she slowly walked through her house en route to her bedroom, softly rubbing her hand up against the picture's that aligned the wall of her hallway. Then placing her purse and other items inside of her room.

Meanwhile, up in the living room, Bre was busy playing with her dolls as Karen stared down at her, mind wandering back to a time years ago, when her first daughter played with her dolls the same way. A single tear escaped her right eye as she daydreamed of that time.

'Boy, how I miss holding you. If only I could see you, just to tell you how sorry I am for not keeping you with me.' She thought to herself as her head and body fell back up against the couch she was seated in. Snapping back to reality and what lay before her, she called out to Sharon. "Are you alright back there, honey?"

"Yes ma'am! I'm just trying to find something comfortable to change into," she answered back as Bre ran back and forth throughout the house, laughing and playing by herself. Not only was Sharon thrilled to be home, but so was her precious lil daughter. Sharon had just changed into something comfortable and sat on the edge of the bed, smiling and admiring her young daughter. She even thought about dialing my number, but quickly changed her mind, when Breanna came up to her and softly rubbed her stomach. "Mommy, is my lil brother okay, inside of your stomach?"

This caught her off guard for a brief moment. She even turned her head sideways as she gazed at her young daughter. "How do you know it's a lil boy inside of my stomach, Bre?"

An innocent, shy little smile emerged onto her face as she simply replied. "Because I saw him last night, right before I went to sleep, mommy. He was rubbing my face as I was talking to him."

Sharon looked at Bre with an uncertain look on her face and then asked her. "How did he look?"

Bre started laughing as she ran towards the bedroom door and then suddenly stopped and turned around to her mother and said. "Mommy, he looked just like the man that Mister Michael was talking to that day in your bathroom, right there." She had pointed to the open bathroom door, that my conscience had first revealed himself at.

Sharon was startled as her mother yelled back to her. "So, Sharon, after all what has happened to you, is the baby okay?" She asked as she walked into the kitchen, stirring about for something to eat.

Sharon didn't want to answer from the back, so after the conversation with Bre, she lazily walked into the living room, when she peeked around the corner of the kitchen. "The baby is fine, mother. But at one time I thought that maybe something was wrong with the baby. But I was reassured once the doctors ran a few tests on me and the baby."

"That's good, what would you and Bre like for dinner?" She asked as she stood in the kitchen smiling. A part of her wanted to reveal her secret, but another part of her wasn't ready to let that out.

"I really don't have an appetite, mom. So let's just order some pizza," Sharon said as she stared at Bre playing with her dolls, sitting in the middle of the floor.

"That sounds nice. I would love to have some pizza right about now, myself," her mother voiced as she walked from around the kitchen, then taking a seat right across from Sharon.

She had just made herself comfortable in one of her leather comforters, when she picked up the remote and turned on the television to see and hear.

"This is Eyvonne Rideout, with the channel eleven evening news. She was a beautiful black woman, who reported on the evening news. "First on news eleven at six this evening. Homicide Detective John Dugan Hatfield of the Orlando Police Department, was found dead inside of his hospital room, earlier this morning. As you all might already know, Detective Hatfield was involved with four other officers in the terrible kidnapping of Ms. Sharon Conoly. He was being held at the hospital under heavy police protection. The doctors and staff were all devastated as to how this might have happened. The hospital at this present time does not know what the cause of death might have been. There has been a full investigation opened into the cause of his untimely death. He leaves behind a wife and five young kids, that now are left without a father or husband. We will have more news of this developing story tonight on the eleven o'clock news."

Sharon's mouth was agape as she looked over at her mother, who was still seated across from her. '*Damn! I can't believe that we killed the wrong muthafucking cop!*'

"What was that dear?"

"Nothing ma, I was just saying that I have lost my appetite for real. That asparagus eating ass cracker is still alive."

Chapter 5
Mind Yo Business!

Mignon, Entyce, Strawberry, and the stunning looking Tameia, were all seated around the pool. Eating and drinking, when Reese walked to the kitchen door with his bags of clothes at his side.

"Hey Entyce, I think ole boy wants to holla at you," Strawberry recited as she saw him standing there, by the door, with a sad look on his face. With what seemed to be a lonely tear, snaking down the right side of his face.

"Who?" Entyce asked as her head swiftly snapped around to witness him standing there.

"Your live-in boyfriend, that's who!" Strawberry blurted out.

"What the hell ever, you mean my ex live-in boyfriend," she replied as she emerged from the pool, dripping wet, trying to conceal her fragile emotions. You see she always had very delicate emotions, from the very first moment she joined the group. I guess you can say that it began the second day of her joining us.

We were all getting ready for a show with the 69 Boyz. We were at the club and waiting for the time they were supposed to go up on stage and dance with them.

Well, when it was time, the girls all went to stand up and that's when I noticed something very peculiar and quite odd about Entyce. So being me, I quickly shouted out to her. "Hey, Entyce, let me holla at you for a minute, please."

With her cute smile etched onto her face she just replied back with. "Sure Mike, is there something wrong?"

By the time she made it over to me, I was like. "Hey, did you know that you're leaking from the back of your ass?"

Her face held a shocked and surprised look on her face as she replied. "No, where? I didn't even feel it."

"Hey Mignon, take her back to the restroom and check and see what's wrong with her outfit." Mignon and the rest of the ladies were ready to go on stage, so she came back at me with. "But Mike, we're all about to go up on stage with the 69 Boyz."

"Not with her leaking from the back of her gotdamn outfit!" I said, just loud enough for her and Entyce to hear me. I didn't want to startle the rest of the crew.

"No problem, Mike, we'll be right back."

Mignon then quickly gathered Entyce by the arm and whisked her away while I stood there, contemplating the girls and their big performance that night. Nosy ass Ms. Kitty walked up to me, arms folded and asked. "What's wrong with Entyce?"

"I have no idea. Didn't I tell you girls to always make sure that your ready and prepared for shows?"

She looked at me all puzzled. "Yeah, the last time I checked, we were all good," she replied in her defense. "

Well not Entyce," I stated as her and Mignon walked back out of the restroom.

Now with a look of sheer concern on her face, Mignon looks at me with those sexy ass eyes of hers and tells me. "Mike, I think we have a slight problem."

"And what's that Mignon?" I asked, with a curious look on my face.

She took a deep breath, then sighed as she said. "I think Entyce has a STD."

"Damn!" Was all I could say as I looked at her, then Entyce. The poor girl was mortified as she stood there looking up at me, hot tears in the well of her eyes. "Okay, let's don't panic here. Tell you what, Kitty get the girls together and you guys go ahead and do your show on stage. Entyce."

She looked at me with those big praline eyes of hers. "Yes, Mike."

"You're going to have to sit this one out. There's no way that I'm going to allow you to get up there on that stage and embarrass yourself, the group and definitely not me."

"I understand, Mike," Entyce uttered with disappointment etched onto her face. But deep down inside, it hurt me more than it hurt her.

The very next day, me and Entyce traveled to the nearest hospital, where it was confirmed that she had an apparent STD but that wasn't what fucked up her emotions. That same weekend we all traveled to Jacksonville for a show. Everything went fine and we were on the way back home, when I got a call. The caller had told me that my apartment had been burglarized, but here is when things became apparent to me about who I let come into my house. We had a chick from Palaka, Florida with us that weekend. She had already knew about my apartment being broken into, why? Because she helped orchestrate the entire thing. On the day when we left, her lying ass claimed she had to go back upstairs and get something. I let her ass go back inside and she left the door unlocked on the way out. I should have double checked, but that's what I got for trusting bitches that I didn't know.

So when we all arrived home, the door to the apartment was closed, after the manager had locked it back after the breakin. But the guys who broke in, found the medical paperwork that Entyce had received from the hospital. To make matters worse, they took her paperwork and plastered it on the door, with a message that read.

We see why you call your whores, The Florida Hot Girls."

But that wasn't all they did. They took her prescription of pills and sprinkled them all around the front of the door for the entire neighborhood to see. Poor Entyce was crushed all over again. Then to make matters worse, one of the local jits that she was fucking stepped up to her and accused her of giving the STD to him as well. I still remember it all, as if it was yesterday...

Back to that day at the pool. They told me that Reese was hurt as far as how bad I didn't know. But once he seen Entyce at the pool, he asked her. "Can I holla at cha for a minute please?"

"Yeah, hold on, let me get this water off of me?" She replied as she stood up. Then looking amongst the girls. "Can you all hold up for a moment while I see what his ass wants?"

"Sure, go handle that, while I turn this music up!" Strawberry yelled as she turned the volume up to the sound of the Quad City DJ's the song was their hit single, *"C'mon N Ride the Train.*

Entyce had wrapped her towel around her waist, when she stood feet away from her ex-man.

"You know that's cold," he remarked as he stood there looking like a sad puppy in the face.

"What?" She asked as she stood there staring back into his face of the man she thought would be her life long partner.

"The way that you talked to me earlier and the way you're just kicking me out. Acting like it doesn't bother you," he spoke as he wiped away the lone tear that had escaped from the well of his right eye.

"What bothers me the most, Reese, is that you're asking me all kinds of questions about what it is I do. Do I ask you questions about where you hang out at all times of the night?"

His head sunk into his chest, then it came back up as he mildly said. "Nah, not really."

"Alright then. So you think it's okay to ask me?"

"But Entyce, listen baby, you know how I feel about your ass," he said as he reached out for her arm.

She angrily pulled her arm away from him, even turning on her heels, walking away. But right before she reached her girls, she turned to him and said. "Not right now Reese, I have a lot on my mind."

"I see how you going to act, so I guess you really want me to leave, huh?"

"Not really, but I think we need some space between us right now. When you get you shit together, maybe we can get this shit we call a relationship back on track."

"Yeah, your probably right. If you need me, I'll be just a call away," he said as he turned and walked away with his feelings tucked into his back pocket.

"Alright Reese. I'll holla at cha later!" She said to him as she threw up the deuces sign. Just when she got back to where the girls were seated, watching. Strawberry just had to be the clown, when she asked. "Damn chick, where's old boy headed to, Band Camp or something?"

All of the girls burst out into laughter, even Entyce cut a side smirk as she uttered. "Funny bitch! Mind yo business, Strawberry, mind yo business."

"My bad, just asking. Don't take it like that, sister."

"Yeah and don't you take what I said like that. Just know that I decided that we needed some space, before things become too toxic for me and him around here."

"What?"

"Nothing Strawberry, girl just chill," Mignon said as she continued to laugh. Minutes later, they all were laughing and having a grand ole time. Drinking and eating, thinking of better times. It wasn't until Mignon heard her phone ringing, that snapped her out of her little funk…

Chapter 6
Stunting and Shit!

She told me that it was around six pm when she walked away from the ladies as she took the call. Once the call was over, she waltzed back over to the ladies with a half smile on her face. "Who was that, that has your ass all smiling and shit?"

"Damn Strawberry, if I didn't know any better, I would think that your nosy ass worked for them crackers! With all the damn questions your flat booty ass be asking?"

"It's not like that, chick. I just happened to notice the smile on your elegant ass face. Hell, I thought that maybe somebody was calling about us making some money or something," Strawberry replied as she turned to walk away, with her feelings, slightly hurt. Mignon saw the hurt in her eyes as she threw her arm around her neck of her dear friend. "My bad, I didn't mean to hurt your feelings."

"Oh yeah, well that's exactly what you hurt," she replied as she allowed herself to feel like she was dearly hurting. "Well this should cheer you and the rest of the ladies right on up then," Mignon recited as her entire face turned cheerful.

"What's up, girl?" Tameia asked as she stood up, pulling her thong bathing suit out of her phat ass Kitty Kat.

"That was ole girl calling from the hospital."

"Nicole?" They all asked in unison.

"Yes girl, who in the hell else would it be?" Entyce shouted as she stared at her dumb friend.

"What did she say, is she alright?" Tameia asked.

"Yes, she's fine. She said that they are releasing her and that she should be ready by the time we get there to pick her ass up."

"That's what I'm talking about, so why in the hell are we still sitting here? Let's go change so we can pick her ass up."

"Hold on there, sport. I'll go pick her up, while you guys stay here and make sure everything is set for a nice welcome back home."

"That's a good idea Mignon, but what about Michael? It's not a party unless his ass is here?"

"I know, Entyce. We'll just have another one, when his ass gets back home."

"Sounds good," Tameia voiced as she went to walk back into the house, swaying her lil thick ass cheeks from side to side. Making sure the girls all got a good look at just how fucking fine she really was…

***

Nicole was released from the hospital around seven thirty, tired and ready to leave. Her mind was bent on heading over to her mother's house and lay low there until she could sort things out. But little did she know it, Mignon and the girls at the house had something different in mind for her. When Mignon arrived at the hospital, the place was still in a frenzy as the cops were running around searching for answers into the horrific death of one of their own. He used to be a good cop, but like many people who are sworn to duty are sometimes swayed by their evil intentions. I guess that's what happened to Detective John Dugan Hatfield. But you who are reading this book, know that he just happened to run into the wrong set of people.

As Mignon rolled Nicole out to her car, Nicole looked back at all the commotion and whispered. "Good luck in finding the culprits responsible for that one."

"What was that Nicole?" Mignon asked as her head leaned down to get a better listen to as what she had just said.

"Nothing chick, just get my ass out of this damn wheelchair and then take me somewhere so that I can get my hungry ass something to eat. I'm fucking starving."

"Yes, Ms. Daisy," Mignon replied as the both of them burst into light laughter. It had been a few days since the both of them had shared a laugh together and for the first time in a long time; it felt damn good.

After gently placing her into her seat, Mignon swiftly made it around to the driver side of Nicole's car. She then turned the key in the ignition to hear the beautiful sound of the engine inside Nicole's car, purring, like a fierce lioness. The sound was music to Nicole's ear, since she hadn't really had much time to enjoy her new pricey automobile. Her face held a wicked half smile as she glanced over at her dear friend who had just turned onto Orange Blossom Trail, headed towards John Young Parkway.

"Girl, you look good as fuck, pushing my new whip!" Nicole shouted as Mignon looked over at her, then sliding her Chanel shades down her face.

"Wait until you see what I ordered myself yesterday from the Benz dealership."

"Nah chick, don't tell me that you're about to cop yourself a brand new Benz?"

Now with a half smirk on her face, Mignon stated. "Yes, that I am hoe! I can't let you be the only bitch around here stunting and shit!"

"Whatever, first of all I'm not a hoe, only one man has ever hit this and we all know who that man is," Nicole spat with attitude while Mignon couldn't hold her full smile back as she merged onto the I-4 ramp, headed towards the Universal Studio exit. Nicole noticed the familiar route and jerked her head over. "Excuse me chick, where are you taking me?" She asked, realizing that she was headed straight back to where it all began.

"Where else would I be taking you hoe? Your black ass is headed back to the crib, that you shot your crazy ass at.'"

"Wait a minute, isn't Mike and Rhynyia still there?" She asked, looking as if she was about to cry.

"No Nicole, they left yesterday. Now relax, you're fine. And besides, Michael knows that I'm bringing you back home. You know that man loves you deeply. It's Rhynyia who had the problem with you, but once I talked to her, she had a change of heart about you staying here or being in the group."

"I can't blame the bitch, hell, I slept with her man and was trying to have his baby as well," Nicole recited as she quietly tried to hold back her emotions.

"I see where you're coming from. But you have to realize, you're part of two groups here. Your presence here means so much to everybody. I just can't believe that you were about to throw it all away for a piece of dick."

Nicole then laid her head back up against her head rest and started sobbing. Mignon didn't notice at first, until she heard the loud sniffling. That's when she slightly turned her head as she drove through the guard shack.

"Nicole, I know your not over there crying about nothing? What's wrong girl, are you in pain or something?" Mignon asked, caring deeply about her friend's pain and suffering. But what she was about to tell Mignon next would cause both of them to sit there and shed a few tears.

"No, it's not that."

"Well what else could it be, you're still in the group and like I just said, Michael and Rhynyia are cool with you being here, back at the house."

In between her tears and sniffling, Nicoled uttered. "It's just so much that I have to contend with. I don't know if you all know this, but I believe Michael came to my room to kill me."

"He did," Mignon quickly spat back.

"What, so I wasn't dreaming?" Nicole asked as her head swiftly turned back towards Mignon.

"No you wasn't. He was sent to kill you by Rhynyia. But once I told her about what you had did for him that night over in St. Pete, she realized what was at stake here and had a change of heart."

"So, you mean to tell me that Mike was really going to take me out?" She asked, a quizzical look all over her face. How could the man who she gave her virginity too want to harm her in any kind of way?

"I don't believe so. You see Nicole, the man actually loves your ass. Like I told the girls, he couldn't kill you if you had a gun pulled on him. The man has some real deep feelings about your silly, lil short ass." Mignon stated as she had just pulled onto our street as Nicole looked down at her flat stomach. Both of her eyes began to tear up again. Within seconds, they flowed like a river down her soft, swollen cheeks.

"Hey, it's okay, why all the tears?"

She slowly held her head up, then saying. "The doctor said that by me being shot, that I lost the most important thing to me at this present time."

Mignon couldn't believe what her ears were hearing. "No Nicole, you didn't?" She sputtered as she pulled into the driveway, then slammed the car in park. But her tears said it all as she grayly turned to Mignon with pain and heartbreak written all over her face. The moment was so serene as you couldn't hear a pin drop inside of that car on that day. She then spoke the awful words that any would be mother would hate to have to tell someone.

"Yes girl, I — L — ossst mmmy babbbby!" The loud scream she let out after that, sent both women over the edge at that moment …

Chapter 7
Red Kool Aid

Hours earlier, back at the Chateau Risque, my wish had come true. After several intense minutes, her uncle couldn't find the picture of Rhynyia's mother, which made me happy. Not because of Rhynyia not finding out, but with this new revelation, I now had at least more time in trying to figure out how I would tell her who her mother was and that I actually knew the woman, even though I was sleeping with both of her daughters. There was no way in hell that I could face the both of them, especially with me knowing what was going on. I had to keep this a secret. And my father always told me that if you wanted to keep a secret, tell it to no one. Not even yourself. Because loose lips, sink ships. And besides, once the cat is out of the bag, it's hard to catch him and place him back inside the bag.

Hurt and disgusted, we all took off for the house. By the time that we had arrived, her father had arrived back home and was waiting to meet the man who had swept his daughter off of her feet. Upon us entering inside the massive luxurious estate, we knew that someone of importance was there in the house, by all of the expensive cars parked outside in the driveway. Just as we were about to enter inside through the side entrance of the vast estate, the funeral director and a few friends were coming out of the house. As all eyes caught a stunning looking Rhynyia and us trying to enter the house, the funeral director was the first one to say something when he saw us.

"Oh my goodness, this must be the ever so beautiful, Princess Rhynyia!" The old balding gentleman shouted, voice loud and booming as he held out his arms for her to embrace him.

"Excuse me, Michael," she uttered as she faintly walked over to greet the gentleman. Once he had his feeble looking arms wrapped around her waist, he gently kissed her on the cheek, while whispering into her ear. "My condolences, sweet Princess."

"Gracious Senor' Francois." She then turned to me and my brother after being released from his grasps. "Oh senor., this is my fiance, Mr. Michael Vallentino and his brother, James Vallentino Jr. They're both from Orlando, Florida."

Senor' Francois looked Firstborn and I over as her father stood in the background, taking everything in. "It's nice to meet the man who has won the heart of such a beautiful woman," he said as I greeted him with a simple smile of my own, then saying to him.

"Why thank you kind sir, the pleasure is all mine."

He then turned back towards her father and said. "I will see you all on Saturday at the funeral." The old man then tipped his black Godfather hat and stepped inside of his elegant looking all black Range Rover. I was standing there admiring the vehicle, when her father walked up behind me.

"So, you're the young man that they call Michael Vallentino?" He spoke as he held out his hand.

"Yes sir and you must be the legendary Pierre Santiago, am I right?"

He then firmly took my hand, while smiling back at me. "I am he, now what has my lovely daughter told you about me?" He asked me as he stood there looking like a carbon copy of the infamous Tony Montana himself.

At first I had to do a double take and step back to gaze at the man, who stood there five foot ten inches and showed no sign of body fat anywhere. His face held all the signs of a well kept business man, with wealth and fame to boost. After a few seconds of me standing there struck by his presence, I simply replied. "Nothing but good things sir." I lied, knowing damn well that Rhynyia had far warned me about this man a while ago.

"Well in that case, I'm very pleased to finally meet the man who has swept my young, beautiful daughter off of her feet." He then greeted my brother as he ushered us all inside.

We were all walking through the house, when he yelled out. "Margarita, my dear!"

"Yes, papi," she answered while walking down stairs, gliding as she walked.

"Me and the fine gentlemen will have one of my most expensive wines out in the garden, before we all sit down for dinner, my darling."

His wife smiled at us, right before she sent one of the servants off to retrieve one of the most expensive wines for us to consume.

"Man, that's the shit I'm talking about, right there!" Firstborn yelped as his eyes grew large with anticipation of his big, dried crusted lips, wrapping around a fine glass of wine.

"Just don't show your black ass!" I uttered, just loud enough for him to hear me, then looking over at Pierre smiling, never losing my cool in his presence.

The young looking servant, who didn't look a day older than nineteen, returned with a bottle of their most desirable wines. Along with some nice, extravagant smelling cigars. After he poured the wine into our individual wine glasses, Pierre lifted up his glass and recited a toast. "To wealth, health and prosperity." Our glasses then went bling through the evening cooling sky. We all brought them down and slowly sipped our glass of wine. That was until I looked over at Firstborn, who was gulping down his glass as if it was a tall, cold glass of red Kool-Aid.

Pierre stood there gawking at my brother, with his eyes enlarging with the sight of my brother gulping down his drink. I quickly nudged the fool, just before Pierre uttered. "Your supposed to sip it, my young friend, not drink it as though it is a glass of cheap beer and you're dying of thirst."

My brother then looked over at me, like. "Damn bro, help me out here."

"Hell, I didn't tell your silly country ass to drink it like you were dying of thirst."

Pierre still had an unusual stare about his face. Then, cutting his attention back over to me. "So your the young black man that has my beautiful daughter knocked up? Not to mention over in Orland, Florida shaking her ass for a few measly dollars?"

Firstborn burst into laughter, while spitting out the remaining portion of his wine, all over his outfit and partially mine.

"Not knocked up sir, but having our child, your first grandchild. Not that I have to remind you of that, sir." I paused to allow him to say something, but he chose not too. He simply just sat there, smiling wickedly at me. "And she desires to dance sir whenever we attend a show or club. Believe you me, it's not something that I wish for her to do," I said as I slow sipped my glass of wine.

"Your right, Mr. Michael, please excuse my rudeness."

"No problem sir, I would feel the same way about my daughters as well.

He then sat up in his chair and came at me with heavy artillery. "So Mister Michael, you have two precious daughters already?"

"Yes sir. Shakina and Aerial," I replied, thinking about my two young girls, who there mothers' kept from being by my side. Then thinking that I had left out the most important one. My name sake, Lil Ms. Mykel Essence Vallentino. Who I didn't even know at the time, would be the one who in the end would continue to control and run my lucrative venture.

Even had Pierre thinking that it was lucrative when he snapped me back to reality with. "So, I understand that you run a very lucrative stripping business back in your part of the country?"

"Yes sir, but I wouldn't say that it was that lucrative of a business, but it does pay the bills."

"I see, since I'm the one who paid for that nice house that you and Rhynyia live in. I must say that I'm somewhat surprised to see that you make sure the mortgage is paid on time, every month."

"So, you're the one who the monthly payments go to?" I asked him as I blew out billows of smoke from the nice smelling cigar.

"Yes, why of course, young man."

"Why thank you, sir and I must say the house is beautiful I might add."

"Thank you, Michael. Now that we have that out of the way, there is something of importance that I would like to ask of you."

'Oh shit, here it comes, the business that Rhynyia begged me to stay away from!' but just as soon as he was about to ask me a question, Rhynyia stepped in with, "Excuse me father, but can I have Michael inside with me for one moment, please?" She was already pulling me from the table before he could answer. This is when he stood to his feet and muttered. "Why of course, my darling, anything for you."

I then walked away while leaving Firstborn standing there with Pierre. Which until this very day, was one of the biggest mistakes I have ever made. It was the worst mistake I had made in my entire life. So severe, that in the end, it would cause many married men to leave their wives and kids behind. It would destroy entire communities and black neighborhoods. Even cause young kids wanting to grow up and be just like the men who sold the devil's work to their parents. In the end, it would even cause my dear brother his life. Because once you sell your soul to the devil, there's no way in hell that your going to get it back. All I can say is, you better hope you can make your peace with Yahweh, before it's too late…

***

Meanwhile, back in Orlando, Mignon and Nicole gingerly walked into the house as the girls all stood in the doorway, screaming and shouting as if they were all at a show or something.

"Welcome Home!" They shouted with glee faces. Nicole's face held up a fake smile as she hugged Entyce, Strawberry and Tameia. Then lying to them with. "Thanks ladies, it's good to be home."

"I know that's right! Are you hungry?"

"Yes Strawberry, Mignon was supposed to take me to grab something to eat, but I guess we talked so much on the way here, that she must have forgot about me and my stomach."

"Yes we did," Mignon said, then asked. "What's that nice ass smell? Smells like chicken wings and fries?"

"Absolutely, Mignon. C'mon let's all eat."

Nicole still seemed a bit weak and feeble as she looked at the ladies and asked. "Excuse me ladies, if y'all don't mind can I eat my wings and fries upstairs in my room? I'm still a bit weak and tired.

"Sure girl, here let me help you," Mignon said as she placed her arm up, so that Nicole could grasp it and then walk upstairs to her room. Mignon had her halfway up the stairs, when Strawberry yelled to Nicole. "If you need anything, I mean anything, just let me know. And oh, by the way, it's nice to have your black ass back home."

Nicole densely turned around, still holding onto Mignon. "Yeah, it's good to be back, apple headed ass girl!"

Strawberry smirked as her lips curled up and quickly came back at her with. "Whatever, shoot 'em up kid!" The room burst out in laughter just as she reached the top of the stairs and witnessed the same spot where she was laying the night she shot herself in the chest. She could hear the faint sound of laughter in the background, but it just couldn't stop the pain; she felt when she saw the spot. The same spot where she lay, almost dead just a few days ago.

The both of them were frozen stiff for just a brief moment. The sight was painful to bare, it wasn't until the silence was broke. "C'mon chick, let me help you get in bed, so that I can bring your food back up to you," Mignon versed as Nicole gazed back over at her.

"Thanks, big sis, I don't know what I would do without you," Nicole softly spoke back, almost in a light whisper.

"Well if that was the case, why did your ass try to leave us?"

It took a moment, then a slight grin emerged onto her face as she said. "Chick, I had a lot going on in my head when I left here the other day. First, it was Michael and the fact of him being with Sharon. Then, there was the fact of me being jealous of the quality time he was spending with her ass. Not to mention him being with Rhynyia too. You know a girl can only take so much, Mignon."

"I guess your right girl. But why didn't you just come and talk to me? See, I knew something was wrong with you when were up in Jasper. I tried to warn Mike about it, but he always just blew me off. We even thought that you had kidnapped Sharon, with the way you were caring on."

They were both seated on the edge of Nicole's bed, talking.

"What?" Nicole asked in a surprised look.

"Yeah girl, we all thought that you had abducted ole girl. Then, we all read the sad letter you left."

"Now, why would you girls think such a thing like that?" Nicole asked.

"Because of the way you were acting. Then, Strawberry told me some crazy shit about you wanting to do something awful to her."

"I hear you, so you see, I did have a lot of shit on my mind. But there was no way that I would or could hurt dear Sharon. Oh by the way, Sharon might just be." She stopped in mid sentence, her breathing had become labored.

"Sharon might be what?" Mignon asked, making sure her girl was alright.

"Chick, when I tell you how she had put together a plan on killing one of them police officers, your not going to believe me."

"So how did it go?" Mignon asked.

"Chick, well first of all the girl had dressed up like a nurse and walked into his room, needle in her hand."

"What was she about to do with a gotdamn needle?" Mignon asked. Nicole then went on with her story of the night that her and Sharon had did away with the officer. Needless to say, Nicole hadn't heard about them killing the wrong officers.

Several minutes later, both females were still seated on the bed, when Nicole said to her.

"I'm glad that you hoes tracked me down and saved my life."

"Yes, that we did, it's a good thing too, because if we hadn't got there when we did. Ole boy would have fucked the shit out of your fine, short ass and then put a bullet hole in your head."

Breathing still a bit labored, she replied. "You know, you're probably right, chick. Thank God that you hoes showed up in just the nick of time."

"Whatever Nicole, your food will be up here in about five minutes," Mignon said to her as she stood up and walked to the door. When she stepped outside and made it back downstairs, Strawberry was over at the bar, fucking up a fat ass plate of wings and fries.

"Damn bitch, you have this kitchen fucked up with chicken grease everywhere!"

"I know, smells good doesn't it?" Strawberry asked as Mignon was looking for her and Nicole something to eat. She had just bent over to get her some wings out of the oven, while Strawberry stood behind her smacking loudly into her ear. "Girl, if you don't get your big headed ass out of my face!"

"What, your gonna hit me Mignon?"

"No, silly ass girl, did you cook enough for everybody?"

"Yes, Mignon."

The sight of Mignon being bent over like she was had Strawberry smiling, showing all of her white teeth. "Damn bitch, keep bending over like that in front of me and I'm going to lick the shit out of your fine yellow ass!" Mignon stood up and turned her head back towards Strawberry before saying. "Whatever, I wouldn't let you put them dick sucking lips anywhere on this fine ass body of mine."

"That's how you feel? Don't worry though, I'm going to get my chance to eat that phat ass pussy of yours one day, just wait and see."

"Girl, move your ass out of the way, so I can take Nicole something to eat."

"Yeah, just make sure you save enough for everybody."

"With all of this mess in this kitchen, I'm pretty sure you cooked enough."

"Yes I did, I just hope you all like my cooking," Strawberry said just as Mignon stepped to the bottom of the staircase. "I'm pretty sure it's all good, Berry. Hey, did anyone of you girls call the other girls to see who were all going with us this weekend?"

"Yes I did, I'll give you the list of names after we all eat," Entyce said as her and Tameia walked into the kitchen for another plate of fries…

Chapter 8
To Late 2 Save Him

Just as soon as Rhynyia and I got out of eye sight, Pierre sat back down, smiling at my brother with an evil eye. I guess the devil knew which one of us, he was going to attack. If only I would have known this, or even seen the play coming, I just might have been able to prevent him from making the most awful decision a man could make, especially when it involved everyone associated with him or me. "So Firstborn, that is your name, correct?" Pierre asked, horns showing.

"Yes sir."

"Do you mind if I show you something that I think that you might like?" Pierre smirked at my brother as he placed his heavy right hand onto his shoulder, leading him away from the table. "Not at all sir, what is it, if I may ask?"

"Why of course. But I believe that you would be better off just seeing what it is that I have to offer to you." Firstborn placed an evil wicked smile on his face, while Pierre led him to what looked like a barn. The structure was big and round, looking just like it held different farm animals inside.

But once Pierre opened the doors, it was more than a makeshift barn that held farm animals. It was the very factory that Pierre Santiago used to manufacture and house his illicit cocaine. My brother would tell me later that the place was laced from wall to wall with cocaine, with about forty females working inside, butt ass naked. With about twenty men with heavy artillery in their hands, guarding the place, all while the naked women carefully packed his delicate merchandise.

Pierre then demurely turned towards Firstborn and asked him. "Now, do you see what I was talking about?"

My brother's eyes were just coming back into focus as he looked at Pierre. "Hell yeah, you have a gotdamn warehouse full of butt naked ass women, packing up that White girl Shiiit, you have more butt naked hoes than my baby brother!"

Pierre laughed at my silly ass brother, before saying. "No Firstborn, what you see in front of you, I call a slight problem. That I think you can help me with."

"How's that?" He asked with a dumbfounded look on his face. He even looked somewhat confused as Pierre stood there watching him. "You see the problem is that I have all of this product and I don't have a way of it getting shipped to places like where you live," Pierre said as he and my brother hopped into a golf cart, with Pierre giving him a tour of the large facility.

"So you want me to help you with this small problem that you have?" Firstborn asked as he took his cigar out of his mouth.

"Yes, my dear friend. I need someone like you on my team to start a new regime over in your neck of the woods."

"I see," he said as he marveled at the vast operation, still shocked to actually see what he had always dreamed of doing.

Minutes later, he agreed to do exactly what Rhynyia didn't want me to do. His simple minded ass made a deal with the devil himself, who was none-other than her ruthless, cold hearted father, Pierre Santiago. The deal was something that he put in front of my brother's face and he couldn't refuse. In the end, he had to agree to pedal Pierre's precious, pure uncut White girl for a cut throat price. And to think, the entire time that Rhynyia had my black ass inside the house, showing their servants how to make fucking brown gravy, Pierre had my brother outside, fucking his entire mental the fuck up. By the time Firstborn and Pierre joined us for dinner, everything was a done deal. The large shipment of drugs were taken to a private air strip and housed inside of the luxury jet plane. I never even knew that the drugs were even stored there, until it was too fucking late.

Now here in the story is where you all should have been paying attention. Remember how Pierre kept emphasizing about selling his drugs in our neck of the woods? Right there is where he is making sure that the potent drug should be sold in the black areas me and you live in. Not one damn time did the man say that he didn't care where the drug was sold, just as long as it was being sold in our neighborhoods. In the end, just like I said in the beginning, his costly drug would be so addictive that it would cause more harm than good. Both me and my brother's life and future would be changed forever, on this day. Damn shame too, because I really did love my brother. If only he would have seen the writing on the wall, he might have been with me all the way up until the end, but life is not promised to the faint at heart. Greed is a terrible sin that will cost you to be placed into a grave, if your not careful. This would be the awful fate of one...

***

That night we had dinner, while Firstborn and Pierre talked throughout most of the delicious dinner that had been prepared for the entire family. It was as if he was marrying his oldest sibling as they both sat at the end of the huge table, conversing. I guess inside of my brother's small mind, his ass was relishing the thought of becoming one of North Florida's biggest drug dealers. He just didn't realize the problem that would come with the title.

After we all finished dinner that night, I could tell the change that was taking over my brother. I actually felt or sensed something different about him, when he cornered me off before we retired off to bed. Rhynyia and myself reached the top of the stairs first, with him following behind us, wine glass in his hand.

"Hey Mike, or should I say baby boy."

"Yeah." I said as Rhynyia and I stopped.

"I have something to tell you," he said, half smirk on his face.

"What's on your mind, Firstborn?" I asked him as I softly spoke to Rhynyia with. "Let me holla at his drunk ass for a quick minute, I'll be with you in a few."

"Sure, bae." she voiced as she gave me a light kiss on the lips, then walked away. I then stood there with my back against the wall, gazing at her ass cheeks as she walked away, then slipping into her room. Once she got to her door, she turned and gave me a wink, before closing her bedroom door. I guess she was enticing me, so that after I finished up with my brother, I could come and be with her.

"What's up?" I asked my brother, seeing him standing there gazing at Rhynyia himself. "Boy she sure looks good."

"I know James, now I done warned you about my queen."

"My bad lil bruh, it's not like that. But hey, listen up. When we get back to Orlando, I'm going to head back to Madison for a while, if you don't mind?"

"No, not at all, that's fine with me. I'm actually surprised that you have stayed with the girls and I as long as you have."

"I hear you, lil bro. I just figured that you needed some extra security, so that's why I stayed as long as I did."

"I hear you. You sure your going to be good?" I asked him as I took his hand, then embracing him as if his ass was leaving right then."

"Yeah baby boy, I think that I'm about to start up my very own business and be just like my business minded baby brother."

"Yeah, whatever. You sleep tight, I'll see your big headed ass first thing in the morning."

"Okay. And oh, before I forget, what about the money we took from those two cops?" He asked, hoping I would say that he could have it.

"Don't you worry yourself about that. I'm pretty sure I can make some good use out of it."

"Yeah right," he versed as he walked away to his room. A light smirk came about my face as I stood there watching him as he walked away,not realizing what he had done, while left alone with Pierre outside.

Now as I sit here some years later, I still have to shake my head from side to side at what he had done. But the sad part about it all, Pierre didn't know what he had created. Years later, my dear brother would tell me right out of his mouth, that the day he agreed to that deal with Pierre Santiago, was the day he wished he would have put a fully loaded pistol to his head and blew his own brains out. For that night would be the last time that I would ever see my brother in the calm and smooth manner in which he was. As he slowly closed his bedroom door, he peeped his head outside of his door and winked his left eye at me, then closing his door. While thinking to himself of how much money he was about to be making as the local hometown drug dealer. But I'm pretty sure that if he knew how many lives he was about to destroy along with his very own, he probably would have done everything a whole lot different than he actually did.

After a few minutes of me standing there, reflecting on what had transpired, Pierre walked down the hallway, coming directly for me. At first I thought that I had did something wrong, that was until he stopped directly in front of me, holding out his hand; while smiling. He then spoke with. "Make sure you sleep well tonight, Michael."

"I sure will, Mr. Santiago and thanks for allowing your lovely daughter to be my wife."

"Well I had no other choice there, did I, Mr. Michael? For it seems as though she loves you with all of her heart. So what was I supposed to do, break it by saying no? You see my Rhynyia has had enough of heartbreak, since she can't seem to find her mother."

I placed my head down, then looking back into his face as I said. "I guess you do have a valid point, sir."

He then reached his right hand into his pants pocket and pulled out a small photograph. "This is what she was looking for earlier at my brother's restaurant." I stood there shocked at the striking resemblance she held with the woman in the photograph. My bottom lip began to quiver as I uttered. "Yes sir, she was looking for a picture of her mother, so that I could search for her when I returned back home."

"Precisely, this is her mother, when you do find her and I know you will, contact me first. I would like to see the woman who broke my heart before she does." He then handed me the picture as I stood there in disbelief. This is when he shocked the hell out of me, standing there. 'You make sure you tell Karen that she can't hide from me forever. And by the way, how is her lovely daughter Sharon doing? You do know her as well, don't you Mister Michael Vallentino?" Before I could answer his question, he suddenly disappeared, just like that. Damn, was his sneaky ass spying on me and my crew? I didn't know, but I was damn sure going to find out…

Chapter 9
Mercedes Benz!

The splendid looking woman in the picture was beautiful and no wonder her and Rhynyia looked so much alike. It was staring me right in my face the entire time, she was her mother. I knew right then that I wouldn't have to look too far for the woman in the picture. The only problem I had now, was that there was no way in hell, I could let either one of them know that they were actually sisters; almost twin sisters. I said to myself as I turned to walk away from the spot Pierre left me at. The last daunting facial expression that I remembered of him was his sinister grin, covering his evil ass face…

***

10:30 am… Orlando, Florida, back at the Vallentino Estate. That's what we called it. All the way up until my foolish ass lost it. That's a story, inside of another story. Don't worry though, you're going to read how and why, later. But not right now.

Mignon woke up that early Friday morning, knowing that she had a very busy day ahead of her, so she needed to get an early start. First, she had to pick up her new Mercedes Benz, from the dealership across town. Then, head over to Robinson's Paint and Body shop to pick up my truck so they could use it for the transportation to Jacksonville for the weekend. The first person who came to mind was her good friend Nicole. Just as she finished dolling herself up, she strolled down to Nicole's room, tapping on the door very lightly. Trying not to wake the other girls.

"Yes, come on in," the lovely voice said from behind the door. "Good morning, Nicole?" Mignon said to her as she pushed the door open, seeing that she was already up, doing her hair. "Hey, I need you to help me run a few errands this morning. Do you feel up to it?"

"Yeah, what type of errands?" She asked as she slightly turned to look at her friend. Standing there in a nice black, tight fitted skirt. "Well first I have to get over to the Benz dealership and pick up my new car. Then, somehow pick up the Denali from the detail shop."

Nicole smiled as she uttered. "No problem chick, but it seems like we're going to need one more driver, so that we can pick up the truck."

"Yep, seems like it doesn't it?" She asked as Nicole nodded her head up and down.

"So who do you think we should ask?" Mignon asked as she stood in the mirror looking at herself.

"I'm your girl!" Strawberry said to them as she peaked her head inside the room, while holding a huge bowl of Frosted Flakes cereal in her hand.

"Damn chick, your ass always has something off in your damn mouth!"

"Whatever Nicole, if that ain't ass ain't careful, the next thing that I'm going to have in my mouth is that fat ass clit of yours!"

Nicole's head snapped around and a smirk emerged on her face as she sputtered. "Try that shit." They all laughed as Strawberry ran to her room to put something more suitable on to wear.

"Well, I guess we have our slight problem solved." Nicole sputtered. "So, how long will it take you to get ready Nicole?"

"Give me at least another twenty minutes."

"Cool, I'll be downstairs waiting on you," Mignon said as she walked out of the room, headed downstairs, leaving Nicole to herself to put together a nice outfit to wear herself. Downstairs in the kitchen, Mignon was bent over in the fridge, busy trying to put something in her stomach, when she heard. "So I see that your ass has purchased an automobile too?" She stood up, all smiles as she replied. "Yes bitch, I ordered me a new Mercedes Benz yesterday. It should be ready round twelve."

"Damn, Nicole has a new whip and now you bitch. I need to get me one. Lord knows that I'm so tired of depending on someone else giving me a fucking ride!" Entyce said as she turned around to walk her half naked ass over to the counter area.

Mignon had a handful of green seedless grapes in her hand she looked over at her girl., sitting at the island bar, pouting.

"Well it looks like your ass has made a start by getting rid of your first problem. Which was your non-working ass ex-boyfriend."

"I know that's right. Now all I have to do is to get my driver license," she stated as she sat, mind focused in on one thing.

"Damn girl, you telling me that your ass don't have a license to drive?" Mignon shouted as she stood there chewing.

"Yeah, I guess it has been something that I guess I never had to do," Entryce replied, while drinking a glass of chocolate milk.

"I see. Well if you need someone to take your ass to the driver's license place, don't hesitate to ask me." Mignon uttered as Nicole stepped into the kitchen with a genuine smile etched onto her face.

"What's good, ladies?" She asked as she stood there dressed in some nice cut off, tight fitted acid washed jeans.

Right along with her cute Florida Hot Girl T-shirt. On her feet she had on a nice pair of Baby Phat sandals. She had to have the most adorable looking feet a woman of her size could have.

"Nothing much girl. Did you know that ole girl here doesn't have a gotdamn driver license?" Mignon spoke as she turned to look at Nicole.

"Yes, I know that all too well. The damn hoe almost went to jail the night that everything went left," Nicole uttered with a side smirk across her face.

"What?"

"Nothing, I'll tell your ass on the way. Now, let's go. I still have to get back here and pack a few things for the weekend."

"My bad," Mignon voiced as she placed her arm around Nicole's neck, headed for the door.

"Hey Mignon, don't forget to fill her ass in on what's going down this weekend!"

"Oh yeah, I gotcha!" Mignon shouted back as she looked over at Nicole.

"Where is Strawberry?"

"Upstairs I guess."

"Here I come ladies!" Strawberry yelled as she began to walk down the stairs, trying her best to prevent from getting left behind.

The three of them had just hit the door, when Tameia emerged from her room downstairs.

"Hey, where is everyone headed off too?"

"Nowhere chick, them hoes just running a few errands before we have to leave for the weekend," Entyce stated as she walked out from the kitchen.

"Oh, okay, I just heard you say something about filling her in about this weekend, has something changed that I need to know about?"

"Nah, nothing has changed," Entyce uttered as her and Tameia stood in the doorway of the house. After she reassured Tameia that everything was good for the weekend, the both of them walked out to the pool area so that they could call the ladies and let them know what time to be ready for departure.

Thirty minutes later, Nicole was pulling her car up to Robinson's Paint and Body when Strawberry leaned her head over the front seat and asked. "Hey, I thought that we were going to the dealer ship first?"

"Don't you worry there, Berry, you'll get a chance to see that bitch as soon as I get her home." Mignon versed as she went to open the passenger side door. Just as her door opened, Jeff Jr. walked out from his office, yelling.

"Break bread, break bread! For it's them bad ass females that they call The Florida Hot Girls!" His face held a radiant smile as he looked at the girls stepping out of Nicole's car.

"Whatever Jeff, what's good?" Mignon asked, with Strawberry and Nicole coming up behind Mignon.

"Nothing, what's up with y'all and where are the rest of those bad ass females that Mike keeps all to himself?"

"We're here to pick up his truck. And I guess all of the other girls are at home getting ready
for this weekend," Mignon stated. "I see. Well the truck is ready."

"Cool, because we are definitely going to need it for this weekend. What's good with them balling ass niggas you be rolling with?" Mignon asked.

"Nothing right now, but in a few more weeks, I think that we're going to need to do another one of them damn shows!" He spoke as he hugged Mignon, while having a giant smile over his face. The ladies knew exactly what to do as they stood there together, outside of Nicole's car, smiling and laughing trying their best to make sure that they were seen by all eyes at the shop.

"Sounds good to us, Jeff. Whenever you guys decide on what it is you all want to do, call Mike and let him know that you and the fellas are ready to break bread."

"Will do and hey, Mignon, lease make sure that I have you and Nicole with me in the VIP room," he said as he continued smiling at the ladies.

"Whatever Jeff, this one here is only allowing one man to hit all of this lil fine ass," Nicole muttered as she went to get back in her car, sashaying her ass cheeks from side to side, making damn sure that her lil bad ass had all the attention.

"Oh yeah Jeff, you might as well hang that up with that one. Mike has her nose wide open," Mignon said as she smiled back at him.

"What? I thought that he was with Sexy Redd?"

"That he is, but you know how that smooth ass niggas get's down. You might as well say that he's with whoever he decides to be with!" Mignon voiced as she turned to get back inside of Nicole's car.

"Damn! That nigga has all the luck!" He said as he handed the keys to the truck to a quiet ass Strawberry.

"Don't worry though Jeff, I don't have a problem with you having me in the VIP room," Strawberry stated with a bright smile, beaming on her face.

"Yeah-yeah-yeah, but with what I saw them brothers putting your lil young ass through the last time, I don't think that I can fit inside of that wide ass pussy of yours," Jeff remarked as Nicole and Mignon burst out laughing.

"Whatever, this pussy stays tight! Believe that!" Strawberry shouted as she walked away to get inside of the truck.

The look she gave Jeff after stepping inside of the truck, was one that had her looking serious as a heart attack. While she sat there in her body, Nicole and Mignon pulled out of the parking lot, headed straight through the light on Old Winter Garden Road. When Strawberry did get herself together, she made a quick left, headed back to Metro West.

"Girl, Jeff has some pretty ass green eyes, don't he?" Mignon asked as she turned her head to stare back at Jeff Robinson Jr.

"They're alright," Nicole said as she kept her eyes on the road, smiling as she thought of the last show she did with him and his big money friends. "And besides those light green eyes of his, he has some long ass paper."

"Yeah, I've heard. Now why doesn't your lil hot ass have any panties on, Mignon?" Nicole asked as she peeped what others dreamed about seeing.

"Oh, your ass saw that, Nicole?" She asked as she made an attempt to pull her skirt down. "Hell yeah chick, I saw all of your lil bald headed pussy."

"That's for my salesman. Since he made me the deal of the century over the phone, I want to reward him by allowing him to see what drives most men wild."

"His ass has to be white," Nicole remarked.

"Girl, how you know?" Mignon asked as she bent over laughing.

"Because, that's just how I got mine. By showing his ass my pretty ass Kitty Kat," Nicole recited while grinning back at Mignon, as she made a left onto Colonial Drive, headed for the Interstate.

"Well I'm bout to show his white ass all of this hot, fine looking pussy, while his ass gives me the keys to my new Mercedes," Mignon said as they both sat there laughing with one another...

Chapter 10
Baby Toe!

Now while those two were off taking care of their business, doing their own thing, the rest of my delightful squad of beautiful ladies, were at home or out shopping; preparing for their deadly weekend. Not having the faintest idea about what was about to take place in Duval county for the weekend. In the end, me and my brother, along with Rhynyia and her sister would be a few minutes 2 late.

First it was the sensuous, tasting looking Lil Kitty, who had her little tart ass busy at home doing what she did other than smoking weed. She was doing her hair and packing a few of her new outfits. She actually was doing more than one thing at once. "Multitasking while talking on her cell phone to the Booty Eating Bandit … my cousin, Richard. Her face held a bright smile as she uttered.

"Richard, I told yo ass that I would see once we get to Jacksonville, now let me go, so I finish doing my hair."

"Okay girl, hey, you didn't tell anybody about how I ate that ass, did you?" He asked as he sat there smiling back into the phone.

At first she rolled her eyes and she sighed into the phone. Then uttering. "No Richard, but I did tell a few of my girls about that fye ass head game of yours!" Right after expressing her sentiments, she had to hold back her laughter.

"Whatever, hell, if they know how fye my head game is, then them bitches are going to want to see how I put it down in the bedroom!" He replied as he reached down and grabbed at his crotch area.

"Yeah, whatever. Boy bye," Lil Kitty said as she abruptly hung up the phone, then saying to herself. *'If them hoes only knew how long that dick is, they would all be just as mad as I was!'*

JK and her crew of gorgeous women were busy over at the Florida Mall, shopping for a few outfits for the long weekend. While Suga Bear and "Chief Smoking Head" Chazz, were at home, smoking on some real nice weed that had a purple bud in the center of it. Their concentration was stifled for a brief minute, when their girl Peekachu shouted from the bathroom.

"Hey Step, where is the laundry detergent? I still have to wash out this cheap ass thong!"

"Under the sink, bitch!" Suga Bear yelled back as she wet her lips and then inhaled the smoke from the blunt. The two of them were so close that their lips accidentally touched each other. "Damn girl! Your chapped, crusty ass lips touched my lips, hoe!" Suga Bear yelled as she angrily stood up and began wiping her lips.

"So what bitch, we're fucking sisters, it don't matter! Now sit your high yellow ass back down and give me a Shotgun!" Chazz shouted as she handed her the blunt, so she could get ready for her anticipated high.

"Whatever hoe, I don't know where those dick sucking lips of yours have been!" Suga Bear replied, laughing as she sat back down. From the bathroom, Peekachu could be heard screaming.

"All I know is that you hoes better save my ass some of that good ass weed!" She was still trying to scrub out her cheap ass thong.

"Hoe, just scrub out that dirty ass thong. We'll save your ass the roach!"

"Fuck you, Step!"

Fine ass Chyna, was at home still sleeping. She would always be the one who waited until the very last minute to get ready. Making sure that she held everyone else up, every fucking weekend.

Chanel was busy at her mother's house, arguing with her mom about watching her lil bad ass baby for the weekend. Something she did every weekend, right before I would come to pick her Weezy Jefferson voice ass up.

By now, we had this one new chick in the group, by the name of Hattie. But for some strange, odd reason, everybody called her lil short ass Heidi. Due to the fact that our African limo driver couldn't pronounce her name correctly. His name was Henry and he called poor lil Hattie, Heidi. He called her this so much, that we all just ended up calling her the same thing. Now the unusual thing about my girl Heidi, was the fact that she was cut from a different cloth. She was okay and all, but when it came to her making her money, she always made it during the wee hours of their shows. Her name actually should have been "Slow Money", because her money came to her real slow. Now that I sit here and think about it, maybe it was all due to her Baby Toe, that sat on her right foot, that sat right on top of her other toes. Which made it a very extraordinary sight to see. The first time that I saw it was at a show in Apopka, Florida.

Some of the girls were in the back, where they dressed in at. It also was where the VIP room was located. For some reason, Heidi needed to change shoes, so she sat her lil black ass down and proceeded to take off her shoes. Well me of course, was seated right next to her, when she placed her foot on my leg and said.

"Ahhh Mike, my feet hurt, could you please rub my feet for me?"

When I looked over and witnessed that fucked up lil baby toe on her foot like that. Boy I screamed like a stuck pig. "Girl, if you don't get that lil fucked up looking foot off of my leg, I know something!" While screaming out with sheer excitement, the rest of the girls just had to see what it was that had me screaming. And when they did see her lil toe, everyone of them girls burst into laughter…

Charlie B had her attractive ass at the nail salon, taking care of her nails and toes. While her counterpart, shopped over at the Magic Mall, looking for some tighter pants, so that her ass could look bigger for whomever she danced for.

Richard and his crew of ladies, had just pulled up to the Magic Mall, to do some last minute shopping. While Entyce and Tameia stayed at the house, packing their individual bags for the weekend. By now, Mignon had her new Five Hundred Series Mercedes Benz, flying down Interstate four, headed back to Metro West. The car was a beautiful foreign piece of automobile, especially with it being cocaine white in color and equipped with a giant sun roof on the top of it. The car came with some nice ass factory rims that actually looked good. But those rims would be changed just as soon as she returned home from Jacksonville. That's if we were to make it back in time. The interior of the car was decked out in all white, with a booming sound system to boot. As she sped down the interstate, you couldn't tell her ass anything. With her long black, Yaki silky hair, blowing in the wind. Instead of the car making her look good, she made the car look damn good, as fine as she looked pushing her expensive ass car down the Interstate.

'If Michael could see me now, he would probably go crazy to see my ass pushing something just as clean as one of his whips!' She said out loud, while jamming to Back It Up Hoe by The Underdawgs.

Meanwhile, Tarshay and a few of the ladies in her small crew, were on their way to the house from Winter Haven, Florida. They needed to get there in just enough time, so that they could ride with the rest of the team. Everyone's girl, Lil Red was busy at her new apartment, making sure she had everything packed, since this was going to be her last show with the group. It seemed as though her and the guy that played ball with the Cowboys had took their relationship to the next level. So she wanted to make this show her last one, not that he expressed to her that he wanted to make her a full time house wife and enjoy the finer things in life. Like travel the world and spend his money, with no regrets. Lil Ms. Strawberry had been back at the house for at least thirty minutes and had just finished packing her belongings, when she stepped out into the hallway. She was looking for Entyce. She didn't see her, so she shouted. "Yo Entyce?"

"Yeah, in here. What's up?"

"Nothing, just making sure you were all ready to go," Strawberry said as she walked into her room.

"Girl, I've been ready ever since you guys left me here earlier, why?" Entyce asked as she walked out from her closet and then flopped down on her bed.

"Nothing, just making sure you were okay," she replied.

"Whatever chick, what's really good?" Entyce asked as she grinned over at her pal.

"Nothing really, just hoping and praying that Michael's damn brother keeps it pushing when they get back.

"Wait a minute, your red ass is telling me that your tired of the dude already?" Entyce asked with a surprised look on her face.

"Yes girl. If I knew his ass was just as freaky as my ass, I would have told him to beat it, after the first time we had sex," she said as she walked over to the window, then pulling the curtains back, so she could peek out of the window.

"Girl, you're funny. Well I guess your ass got what you asked for. Remember, you were the one who said that you wanted to be in their family, ole silly ass girl."

"Your absolutely right, but I didn't know that all his horny ass wanted to do was fuck. And I don't mean once or twice during the day, this nigga wants it all the damn time, even in the early hours of the morning."

"Well at least your getting some and besides, he seems like he really likes your silly ass," Entyce said as she sat on her bed, talking to the back of Strawberry, who seemed to be preoccupied by something outside of the bedroom window. She was so gone, that she didn't even hear the last comment Entyce had spoke. I guess her attention was now being focused on the police issued sedan, sitting across the street, looking directly at the house. "Hey, did you hear what I just said?" Entyce asked as she began to sense that something was amiss.

"You might want to come see what I see."

"What?" Entyce asked as she hastily jumped up off of her bed.

"Right there, please don't tell me that those are police detectives, watching the house?"

Entyce peered out the window as if she was an eagle, watching its prey before the attack. "Damn! It does look like it's them damn boys!" She said as she closed the curtains, then looking over at Strawberry.

"What's up Entyce? What do we do now?" Strawberry asked, sounding as if she was a bit scared.

"Hold on Berry, I got this. Where is my phone?" She asked as her head went on a swivel, in search of her phone.

"How am I supposed to know, it's your damn phone," Strawberry uttered as she frantically pranced the room.

"Here it is, got it. Just be cool, while I call Mignon."

Mignon was just passing under the overpass on the Interstate as she felt her phone vibrate up against her thigh. Her phone had rang at least two times as Entyce patiently waited on the other line.

"Answer your damn phone girl," she uttered as she stared out of the window.

"Hello."

"Mignon."

"Yes, Entyce, what's up? Is there something wrong back at the house? She asked, her intuition alerting her that something actually was wrong,

"Girl, I think we have ourselves a problem," Entyce spoke, sounding as if she might be worried.

"What kind of problem?" Mignon asked as she pressed the volume button on her steering wheel, causing the music to go down.

"Looks like there are two police detectives here, watching the house from across the street."

"What?" An alarmed Mignon shouted.

"Two got damn police detectives!" Entyce screamed back into the phone.

"Gotdamn!" Was all Mignon could muster as her mental flew out of her driver side window...

Chapter 11

The dull grey colored police sedan was parked several blocks down the street, away from the house; but you could still get that vibe that they were watching our particular house. It took Mignon about ten minutes to get back to the house. Once she passed through the guard gate, she bent a right onto our street, then slowed down as she came up to the sedan. Both officers were caught off guard as she pulled up, then sliding down her window and saying. "Excuse me officers, is there a problem here?" The lead detective fumbled around with his cup of coffee, from Starbucks, causing half of the hot Java to spill all over the seat as he quickly sat up in his seat and said. "Not at all ma'am, we we're just here observing some nuisance complaints about one of the homes here on this block."

"Oh, that's strange, no one has said anything to us about any problems," Mignon said as her face held a serious glare.

"There's no need to alarm yourself with anything, ma'am. We have been here all morning and haven't heard one peep. Which means that our job here is done. Consider us on our merry little way," the round face detective said as he looked from Mignon back to his partner.

"Why thank you officer, it's good to know that we're being protected by Orlando's finest. Prick!" She mumbled under her breath as she gave her high powered automobile some gas, headed towards the house, with none other than Nicole close behind her. When she pulled into the driveway,

Nicole pulled her car right behind hers. She quickly placed her car in park, then stepping out of it, with a quizzical look on her face.

"Hey, what was that all about back there?" She asked, standing beside Mignon, watching the detectives drive away.

"I have no idea, but with everything that has been happening around here lately, there's no telling what's going on, girl."

"That serious huh?" Nicole asked as she turned to stare at the back of the cops car, slowly driving away.

"Yes girl and I forgot to tell your ass that we had to go back to Daytona, so that we could handle something of importance."

"Why?" Nicole asked as they both stood side by side. "I guess you haven't been watching the news lately." Mignon remarked.

"No, what? Was I supposed to or something?"

"Yes, silly ole girl. Remember that damn lady that shitted on us in the fucking bathroom, back at the gotdamn Red Lobster. Right before we took care of old boy?"

"Wait a minute, oh okay. Yeah, I remember."

"Damn chick, it hasn't been that long and you act like you can't remember. But the lil short thick ass bitch, went to the cops."

"No and did what?"

"What do you think her white ass did? Her lil chunky fat ass gave them people a very good description of how we all looked."

"What? How in the hell could the bitch remember how we all looked?"

"Wait a minute," Mignon said, then continued with. "Now that I think about it, all she had to do was look at the footage of all of us being there and then put two and two together."

"Damn, you don't think that those cops were here for that, do you?" Nicole asked with a bit of concern etched over her gorgeous face.

"They couldn't be here for that, if so they would have had half of the gotdamn police department here with them. I have no idea as to why they were here, but we sure as hell will find out sooner or later." She stopped and closed her car door. Then standing up right she said. "So we better be prepared for whatever happens next. Now let's go meet up with Entyce and Strawberry so we can hatch out some type of plan."

"Damn! I get shot and leave here for a couple of days and you hoes go out and fuck up everything!" Nicole said with a side smirk on her face.

Mignon turned to look at her dear friend and placed a smirk on her face as she uttered. "Shut the hell up, trick, bring that ass!" Both of the ladies walked inside of the house, not even seeing the small pea shaped head black guy in the back seat of the police cruiser. But someone else did. And that someone was just about to spill the beans about what she saw. What she had to say, would almost crush me and those lovely ladies, known as the Florida Hot Girls...

***

Mignon and Nicole couldn't even make it to the door good as Entyce and Strawberry hit them at the front door with. "So, what's really good? Who were they and why were they here?"

"Damn Strawberry, calm the fuck down!" Mignon growled back as she stepped inside and closed the door behind her. "Where is Tameia?" She asked as she searched the foyer, then walking into the kitchen, still searching. She didn't want Tameia to hear something she wasn't supposed to hear.

"Why Mignon, were they here for her lil short ass? I knew her lil fine ass didn't have a fucking green card."

"No Strawberry, they were not here for her. Now, where is she?"

"She's in her room, Mignon, why, what's up?" Strawberry asked, really overreacting right about now.

"We have to make sure no one hears what we talk about! Now everybody follow me out to the pool house. That's the most secure place around here to talk."

"Fine, right behind your sexy ass, Boss Lady."

Mignon turned her head around, this time she wasn't smiling as she cut an evil stare at Strawberry and said. "Alright you, with that Boss Lady shit, Strawberry! If this shit hits the fan, we all will be working for the Boss Lady, for a very long fucking time! Let me ask you something? Are you cool with a bitch licking and fucking your ass all day?" Mignon asked her, then right before she could answer the question, she placed her index finger on her cheek and stated. "Oh, wait a minute, I forgot, your freaky ass likes women and men."

"I sho do, like I said before. One day I'm going to get that chance to lick that fine ass of yours, right along with the pussy. Hell, why not do it in the privacy of our own two woman cell?" Strawberry asked, with a smirk of her own.

"Whatever bitch, I ain't going to no one's prison. Now whatever the rest of you hoes want to do, is all up to y'all ass," Nicole said as she stood there, serious as a heart attack.

"I hear you chick, now let's stop with the bullshit, to the pool house."

"I'm right behind you Entyce, lead the way," Mignon uttered as they all turned and walked out to the pool house.

Just as the cops had got out of the gated community, their short ass informant slowly eased up in the backseat of the cruiser.

"Hey, are you two guys sure that they didn't see my black ass sitting back here?"

"I'm positive. Everything is okay. Now are you sure that you have information that can put his organization behind bars for a very long time?"

"Yes, I know I can. Just as long as you guys can assure me that I'm protected."

"That's not a problem. We told you that we are going to put you in police protection, twenty four hours a day, seven days a week. You will be protected at all times, just as long as your willing to testify against Mr. Michael Vallentino and the women that live with him," the lead detective said as they stopped at a traffic light.

"Yes sir, to the fullest of my ability. Now, what about the reward money?" Their informant asked as he sat up in the backseat of the cruiser.

"We'll talk about that later. We just want to make sure that your good and safely hid away from the public.

"Okay, thanks for the concern."

"Don't mention it, that's what we do. Now we're going to take you to the house, for you to make yourself comfortable. Whatever it is you need when you get there, go ahead and think of it now, so we can get it approved through the department.

"No problem," The Rat said as a smile came across his face...

**

By the time the police cruiser had driven to the plush, lavish community, their informant had dozed off into a very deep sleep. The officer on the passenger side noticed it, due to the loud snoring of the tired informant passed out."

"Good, now his lil black ass won't be able to call and let anyone know where he's being hidden away at," the driver uttered as they pulled up to a nice four bedroom villa. Just as they pulled up close enough to the two car garage door, the driver hit the button on his sun visor, releasing the door, then slowly driving the car inside.

The nice stylish villa was located right outside of Orlando, Florida. Enshrouded neatly away inside the small town of Lake Mary, Florida. Right next to the robust town of Sanford, Florida. This was the perfect place and area to hide someone, if that someone was willing to testify on the very same people that had taken his black ass in.

You see, when his ass first arrived at our humble abode, one night we had a show over at this small club, right off of Colonial Drive. The club was a small island club, right next to a large plaza. This cute island lady wanted to sauce up her club, so she hired the girls and we showed up. But unfortunate for one of the girls, this night would be horrific for her and her new found boyfriend. At the time of all of this taking place, I was inside the club, making sure the girls were making their money. I might add though, the club was slow, which meant the money was slow. So there I was with my girls in a club that provided no money for them at all. Low and behold, one of their favorite customers showed up this night. His name was Big Al. Big Al was a cool laid back nigga, who had a side kick, by the name of Pinky, who always wore a gold cut diamond necklace with Pinky from the cartoon show Pinky and the Brain on it. When I asked Big Al about his partner's chain, he would always tell me that he was the brain and his partner was Pinky…

Chapter 12
Big Al and Pinky!

Now on this particular night, when the girls and I were at this show, what would transpire next, should have alerted me then, to not fuck with this certain guy. No, the guy wasn't Big Al, nor his partner, Pinky.

It just so happened to be the guy that my girl Entyce fell head over heels for. You remember when I told you in the beginning that her live-in boyfriend was one of the dancers for the group called The 69 Boyz. Well on this night, two of their security guards happened to be at this show. So while me and Big Al were outside the club talking about doing a show together, my girls and his girls, doing a real big show. Right when we were about to finalize the deal, one of them security guards walked up to me and said. "What's up, Mike?"

"Nothing much, what's good, Big Fella?"

"I was just about to ask your cool ass the same question," the guy said to me, then looked over at Big Al. "What's good Big Al?"

"Nuttin'. What's up with y'all?"

"Nuttin, just out here chilling. Let me ask you something though," the big guy asked.

"Go head, I'm all ears," Big Al responded.

"I just got word that that nigga name Reese is inside the club," the big guy stated.

Big Al immediately looked over at me, while he laced his blunt with what looked like crack. "I have no idea, you have to ask my man, Mike that."

"Yo Mike, is Reese up inside the club with your girls?" My face held a quizzical look as I replied back with. "Yeah, his ass is in there with his girl and the rest of my girls."

Just as I said that, out walks Reese. His head was down and he didn't see the security guards. But when his head came back up and he witnessed the 69 Boyz big ass bus there, something inside of him clicked. His eyes got buck and his feet went to haul ass. But just as his lil sneaky ass turned around, someone grabbed his ass from behind.

"Oh no you don't, my friend! We got that ass now!" Another guy remarked as he picked lil ass Reese up off the ground, his lil ass, legs and feet were dangling as he struggled with the guy.

"Yo man, put me down, please. Come one man, put me down!" Reese shouted, but to no avail. Whatever his ass had done, had come back to haunt his ass on this night. Big Al and I just stood there as the other two security guards held open a trunk from someone's car.

"Put his black ass in the trunk!" The man did as he was told. Now while this was taking place, I run back inside to ask Entyce what in the hell was going on. But her ass was all in tears by the time I had got inside. I guess someone had already told her what was going on outside. This is when I looked at her and asked. "Yo Entyce, what is going on with your man and shit?"

She looks up at me, snot and tears oozing down her face. "I don't know Mike, but you got to help him, before they do something terrible to him." She managed to say.

"What in the fuck you think that I can do?" I asked. Hell I was fearing for my life, just as well as his ass was.

"I have no idea, Mike, but you're the leader of this group and he's part of our big ass family," she stated.

"Alright, let me go out here and see what's up." I versed as I turned to go back outside. Now be mindful, that the Murder Queens hadn't been formed as of yet at this time. So, it was just me. So right before I step outside, I turn and tell Ms. Kitty, to stay put and to not let any of the girls walk outside behind me. She looked at me with those cute ass eyes of hers and said something that still sticks in my head to this very day. "You just make sure you're good. You're my heart Michael and I would hate to lose you over some dumb ass shit that Reese has gotten himself into." At that moment, Ms. Kitty had my heart, right in the palm of her hand.

"I'm good, Ms. Kitty. I promise to be right back," I said to her and then kissed those soft ass lips of hers. I mean her lips were just as soft as her ass cheeks.

When I got back outside, the guys had the trunk close, with Reese inside begging to get out.

"Hey my man, what's up? He's with us, so whatever he did, I'm sure we can straighten it all out."

The biggest of the two security guards walked over to me, face holding a very stern look on it. He then says to me, "Yo Mike, listen. This has nothing to do with you and your girls. This is all on him. You see a while back, his black ass broke into the bus right here and stole half of the clothes that Vann and some of the other members purchased on tour."

"Word," I said, puzzled look on my face.

"Yep, now his ass has to pay for what he did," the guy said to me as Big Al walked up behind me and whispered into my ear.

"Yo Mike, leave it alone. Ole boy got an ass whipping coming. He even stole some of my brother's shit." His brother danced for the 69 Boyz as well as Reese did.

"Oh yeah," I said as I turned my head back in his direction. "So, I guess he made his own bed, that he has to now sleep in." Big Al just put some fire to the end of his blunt and lit it, while the two big husky security guards got into the same car that Reese was held kidnapped in.

"You want to hit this, Mike?" Big Al asked.

"Nah, I'm good, son," I replied as a part of me really felt bad for Reese. Even though he had only been with us for a few weeks, at that time he was still a good friend. Now that he was gone, I had to go back inside the club and tell Entyce the bad news.

"Hey Mike!" Big Al shouted out to me as I walked away.

"Yeah, what's up?"

"Look at it this way, now with his ass gone, that's one last problem you have to worry about!" My lips curled up, due to what he said. Leaving still with a bad feeling about what they were about to do to the poor guy.

"Yeah, you're right, Big Al." Was all I said as I turned on my heels and walked into the club. Just as I got to the door, Entyce was there waiting for me.

"So what happened Mike, did you save him?" Her eyes were bloodshot red from crying so hard and long.

"No Entyce, they said something about him stealing some clothes from the group."

"Oh no, there going to kill him!" She screamed as her head fell into my chest. All I could do was to try my best to somehow console the poor vixen.

As we both stood there, I couldn't figure it out to save my life. Here she was crying over some dude that she barely knew. Hell, get over it and move on, but not Entyce. I guess she had been hurt so much in her young life, that she wanted to hold on to any man that showed her ass love. I had been standing there letting her cry on my shoulders when I guess Ms. Kitty didn't like the fact of another woman being in my arms. So her lil jealous ass walked up to us and said. "Excuse me Mike, I'll take it from here. Besides, there seems to be a nice crowd in here now."

I looked around the small club and did notice that the crowd had enlarged.

"Go on bae, handle your business. Make sure these hoes are making their money, because I don't want to hear nothing about their ass didn't make no money tonight, because the club was small." Ms. Kitty continued to say as I stood there, stiff.

"Yeah, you're right. Let me go tell these niggas to break bread!"

"I know that's right!" She said to me as she took a hold of Entyce's hand and led her to the bathroom.

Minutes later, her and Entyce were dancing on the dance floor, like nothing had happened. That night after the club, all was silent as we drove home. I had just dropped off the last girl, when we pulled into the parking lot. I made sure all of them had their bags and then proceeded to walk to the apartment. We were just about to walk upstairs, when I heard someone calling my name.

"Mike, hey Mike," the voice sounded like the guy was whispering.

"Did anyone else hear that?" I asked as I stopped dead in my tracks.

"Yeah, sounds like it's coming from over there." Entyce was the first person to say something.

"Yeah, who is it?" I yelled as Reese whispered back.

"It's me dawg, is the coast clear?"

"Who?" I asked, still not seeing who it was that was calling me.

"Mike, I think it's Reese!" Entyce shouted and just like that, he emerged from the darkness of the stairwell.

"Yo son, it is your ass, how did you escape?" I asked as Entyce ran over to a tired and battered Reese.

"I'll tell you all just as soon as we all get inside. Entyce and a few of the other girls, then went to his side and helped him up the stairs. Once safe and sound inside, he told us how he had escaped. He claimed when they opened the trunk, his ass leaped out and took off running. Right up until this very day, I still say if he hadn't done what he had done, he might not have been able to tell his side of the story.

Now here it was a few years later, that his ass found himself in the back of a police cruiser, sleep.

"Hey you back there, we're here!"

Detective Frank Mease voiced as he placed the car in park, then stepping outside to stretch his long, heavy legs.

"Ahh man, I must have passed out. Where in the hell are we?" Their passenger asked, while wiping the sleep away from his weary eyes.

"Looks like home sweet home. If you ask me, by the looks of things, your ass is living better than the both of us are," Detective Paul Steaphanoski replied as he stepped outside and slammed the door.

"Wow, you can say that again! Who lives here anyway?" Their informant asked as he stepped outside of the car, stretching his legs. Then yawning and scratching his nasty snitching ass at the same exact time.

"No one but you sir, now follow us so we can get you familiarized with the surroundings of your new place. Or should I say, your new home."

He couldn't begin to fathom that such a nice home was all his. "So you mean to tell me that all of this belongs to me and only me?" He was so caught up with sadness, that he wanted to shed a tear. He never had a place of his own and now, for him to be situated in such nice surroundings, he was beyond excited. His ass was in sheer disbelief.

"Yes sir, all this for now, belongs to you. That is as long as this investigation is pending. If you ask me I would drag this thing out as long as possible," Detective Stephanoski recited as the three gentlemen opened up the door, then walking inside to sheer beauty.

"You betta believe it!" Their informant uttered as he walked inside with the detectives, looking around at how beautiful the house was on the inside. He couldn't believe his eyes a she stood there in awe. Marveling at how nice the place looked. For a moment there, he actually thought that his black ass was dreaming…

Chapter 13
Singing Like Michael Jackson!

The four ladies were all seated in the pool house, imprudently listening to Mignon's conversation on the phone with her people on the inside. "So, your telling me that you have no idea why the police were staked out at our house today?" Mignon asked the person on the other line. "No, it sure as hell wasn't anyone from Daytona Beach. The lady and family who you guys have under wraps is scared as fuck. The bitch ain't talking to no one, I mean no one!"

"Good. Well, I wonder what in the hell is going on? Someone has to fucking know something," Mignon replied. "Did you guys get a good look at where the cops came from?"

"What do you mean?" Mignon asked her inside guy. "Were they from Orlando Police Department or what county were they from?"

"I don't fucking know, they just looked like some ordinary fucking white officers!" Mignon versed back into the phone with attitude.

"Hey, wait one fucking minute. Those cops looked like they were from Orlando," Entyce said as she stood to her feet, then walking to the door of the pool house. All eyes were glued on her as she stood with her mouth wide open. Then placing her hands on her hips.

"How would you know that Entyce?" Strawberry asked as a smirk ran across her face.

"Because, if I'm not mistaken, I saw what looked like an Orlando Magic sticker on the front of the car."

"Okay and what in the hell does that have to do with any fucking thing, Entyce?" Mignon asked as she sat there staring back at her friend. That's when the person on the phone said something.

"Hold on, she might have something there, Mignon. Okay, tell you guys what. Let me do some checking, I'll call you back just as soon as I hear something."

The phone went click, just as the ladies heard a light knock at the door of the pool house.

"Shhh! Yeah, who is it?" Nicole shouted through the door. "It's me, can I come in please?"

"Damn! Now what does this lil chick want?" Mignon whispered to the ladies.

"Ahhhh, we're kind of busy right now, can it wait Tameia?" Entyce yelled back as she stood guard on the door.

"Not this," she uttered as she barged inside, damn near pushing Entyce out the way.

The ladies all remained seated, that was all but Entyce, who stared down at Tameia and uttered.

"Damn bitch! I guess it couldn't wait, huh?"

"Nah, I just thought that you guys would like to know that the police cruiser you all watched leaving the neighborhood had someone sitting in the back seat of the patrol car."

"What? And how do you know we were watching a police cruiser?"

"Now Mignon, just because you walk around here thinking that your the sharpest tool in the tool shed doesn't mean that you are. I've suspected you ladies up to more than just dancing for a very long time now!"

"What are you talking about, Tameia?" She then turned her head in the direction of Nicole and said.

"Nicole, please be for real. Just like I said, you ladies are into just more than dancing. You ladies can actually be like some super hero type bitches with the way you all are dancing one minute. But then you four disappear and then come back and save either Michael or one of the girls in this group."

She had said a lot. Even catching their attention. "Okay, so tell us what or who it was in the backseat of their car." Mignon asked as Tameia looked over at Entyce and then pointed her index finger at her.

"Her ex-boyfriend. And by the way it looked, his lil short ass was singing like his ass was Michael Jackson at one of his sold out concerts...

***

While in the midst of all the turmoil that the ladies were going through back over in Orlando, you would have at least thought that they would have given me a call or something. You know, to let me know what was transpiring back in their neck of the woods. But no sir, not my precious ladies. They kept all this from me. I guess trying to let me know that they could handle just about anything, without me stressing over it. Or maybe they figured that I was going through a lot, since I was with Rhynyia and her family, during their time of grief and pain, not to mention suffering over the loss of Prince Naheed...

The mid evening sun over in Puerto Rico wasn't as humid as what I was accustomed to back at home. So it didn't bother me while out shopping for something to wear to the funeral. As we walked to and from, it dawned on me that I had just left one funeral and was about to be at another one. This would be the last funeral that I would be a part of, for a long time. Mainly because I always hated to see another person leave, due to it being by the hands of someone else. I said all of this to myself while browsing through the different clothing stores.

Minutes later, we all stopped off in a nice lil plaza that was surrounded by nice cultural artifacts that made your imagination run wild. I was taken away for a brief moment, that was until my baby shouted out to me. "Michael, do you even know what type of suit you're looking for?"

"Nah, not really." Just by gazing at her made me ask myself, how in the world would I be able to keep her from seeing the picture of her mother? And then, how could I tell her who her mother or sister was? I continued staring at this beautiful creature, realizing that I had seen all the signs and even striking resemblance some time ago. But being me, I put all those notions to rest, not realizing that one day this would sure to happen. Now that I was staring at her, I could see how they all looked exactly alike. I would have to put on my best act ever, if I wanted to keep their identities a secret. Because if they were to find out, it just might cause me to lose both of them. All of this was spinning through my mind as I dared not to lose either one of them, but that would only mean certain disaster for me if my dumb ass thought that I could have both of them.

All this crowded my mental while walking and pondering, when I looked over at my country ass brother. Then it dawned on me. *What if this nigga became jealous of me and told both of them my secret? Ah, hell nah! I now had to get rid of his ass, before he destroyed everything I had.'* I said to myself as I looked back in front of me. My brother was like that. If things didn't work out for him, he didn't want it to work out for anyone else. We all call that being selfish and that's exactly how his country ass was.

"Michael, what are you doing back there? Please try to keep up!" Rhynyia yelled at me as I was dragging behind her and her bodyguards. I guess I was so far behind, because I had guilt, written all over my face.

"My bad, baby girl." I shouted back as I hid my inner feelings, with a coy smile, then catching up to her, with her looking over at me.

"I hope you have what type of suit you want to wear to the funeral in mind. Because this is the last store on the island," she spoke to me as we walked hand in hand into the high dollar men's fashion store.

Just as soon as we all entered into the store, I spotted the perfect suit. It was a nice white Julio London suit. I swiftly turned the suit around to see the price tag and was like.

"Damn, this suit is expensive as hell!" I didn't realize how loud my voice was inside the store, since we were the only customers inside. So I swiftly threw my hand up over my mouth.

"How much is the suit, Michael?"

"If my eyes serve me correct, the price tag says, two thousand dollars."

She now stood behind me with her arms folded across her small belly bump. With a smirk smeared across her face, she says. "That's it Michael, stop acting like you don't have any money."

"I don't, not like that," I quickly replied.

"If you want the suit, go ahead and get it. You know I'll pay for it."

A very large smile appeared on my face as I looked around the store and said. "Where is the sales associate?"

"I have no idea, hold on a minute," he said, then shouted out. "Raoul, where is the sales manager?" She said to her bodyguard, who immediately turned around and began searching the store for the man, who emerged from behind the counter, seconds later.

I swiftly spotted him from the corner of the store, then asked him. "Excuse me sir, do you have this particular suit in my size?" The short Italian looking man looked me over, before saying.

"No sir, we would have to tailor make the suit for you, sir."

"And how long will that take sir?" The small frail man laid eyes on Rhynyia as he walked closer to me, then whispered.

"Oh, I'm so sorry, Princess, I can have it ready for him, immediately."

"Say less my man," I said with a side smirk on my face. I was about to be the flyest nigga in town with that Julio London suit draped over my chiseled body frame … at least that's what I thought, right on up to the actual day of the funeral. How was I to know that Pierre Santiago had the same taste in fine clothing as I?

Chapter 14
Man in the Window!

He then went straight to work as he began measuring me for my suit. And to make sure there were no interruptions, Rhynyia's four huge henchmen placed the closed sign on the store window, until he was done. I knew then that Rhynyia was more than just a Princess, she was the shit, wherever she went over in her part of the world. The tailor had my suit ready within an hour as I marveled at how nicely it fit on my chiseled body. The suit had to be the nicest suit that I had ever owned. I liked the suit so much that before I left the island, I had the tailor make me ten more Julio London suits just like the one I had. All in different colors if I might add.

Just as we were about to walk out of the store, the lil Italian gentleman stopped Rhynyia and said to her, "I'm so sorry to hear about the death of your brother. It all came as a shock to us when we heard the terrible news."

She hugged the frail looking man as she whispered. "Thank you, do you have any idea who might have did this awful thing to my brother and caused our family so much grief and sorrow?"

The man began to shake his small head from side to side, as he uttered. "I would love to help you Princess, but right after they found his body, some of your fathers men came by here and told us to not open our mouth's about anything."

She held an unusual look on her face as she asked the man. "Now why would he do something like that?" At that moment he looked as if he should have just kept his mouth closed. But did say, "I have no idea, Princess."

"So, what do you know?" She asked, now looking down at the small man.

"All I know is that your brother's murder will be a mystery until someone finds out who killed him," he replied as he walked his narrow slumped over body behind the cash register and deposited the large amount of currency that Rhynyia had given him for the suits. I could see the hurt and pain in her eyes as she whispered to me with,

"His ass knows something. And I'm going to find the fuck out!" She damn near ran behind the man as she pleaded with him for answers.

'Senor' I beg of you, if you know anything or the smallest detail about his death, please let me or my family know!"

"I will, Princess, trust me, I will," he said as he held his right hand over his heart, then patting his chest as to show her a sign of peace and solidarity. But just when we got to the door and her henchman outside the store, he whispered, "Princess, now you are the one with all the power. And only you can find out who killed Prince Naheed." She just shook her head up and down and then turned on her heels. We then walked away with Rhynyia looking more confused than before she did when we arrived. As we got back into the Range Rover, I happened to notice a suspicious looking man, gazing at us from the window above the store, but thought nothing of it as the driver sped away, headed back to the house.

As he sped back throughout traffic, she laid her head on my shoulder and then closed her eyes. Trying to somehow forget about the unwanted pain that she was feeling from the loss of her brother.

Since I had been with her on the island, she hadn't spoke of him that often, until that very moment inside of the clothing store. While sitting there holding her and comforting her, I had to ask myself. *Should I tell her about the person I saw staring out of the window at us or should I just keep quiet?* ' In the end, I kept my mouth closed, because in the end, whatever my decision, it would only be a matter of time before we all knew who the man in the window was ...

With the caravan of black Range Rovers headed back to the estate, the suspicious looking man walked down the stairs of the clothing store and violently pushed the old Italian man up against the wall with so much force; that the poor old man winced in agonizing pain.

"Did you tell them anything about her brother's death?" The well built Puerto Rican man asked the store owner as he clutched him up under his neck, lifting his small ass up off of the floor. Causing his small feet to dangle from underneath his small frail body.

"No, I swear to you, that I didn't say anything to the both of them! I was told not to speak of his death!"

"So, why did you even offer your condolences, Chulo?" The man asked with angry veins popping all over his disturbed looking face.

"Because she's the Princess of the royal family. What type of patriot would I have been not to offer my sympathy to the Princess at a time like this?" The small man replied while hanging from the wall as he was a picture without a frame. The man slowly lowered the man, then saying to him as he brushed the man off. "Please forgive me senor', I meant no harm to you. I just have to keep what we all know as our little secret as long as I can. You do understand, don't you?"

"I understand sir, I feel the same way as you do."

"I would certainly hope so senor' Chulo, for I would hate for the same fate that happened to Prince Naheed to somehow happen to you or anyone and your immediate family." The man said as he walked to the entrance of the store, with one of his nice, expensive smelling cigars, held in his hand. For he as well had to prepare himself for the burial of one of his family members. Making sure that no one else knew of his dark secret, of who actually killed Prince Naheed…

***

Silence overwhelmed the pool house as the girls all stood there looking at Tameia. The tension in the small room wasn't broken up until Entyce came back at her with.

"What was that?"

Tameia took her time, while gazing back at the girls, not frightened by any of them at all. She made sure she stood her ground. "Like I just said, your lil short, stinky, snitching ass ex-boyfirend was sitting in the backseat of that car, looking as if his dirty ass was singing like his ass was Michael fucking Jackson!"

"Damn!" Mignon voiced as she stood up.

"So, now are you ladies going to enlighten me on what's going on around here or just keep playing like my name is Willie Lunchmeat?"

Strawberry hadn't said a mumbling word, that was up until now, when she asked. "Willie Lunchmeat? Where is his ass at right now? Now that you have brought his name up, my ass is hungry than a muthafucka!" Everybody turned towards her ass and said in unison. "Shut up, girl!"

"What, can a sister get something to eat around here?"

"Not now Strawberry, you see how things are about to get real complicated around here."

"Yeah, I see. So what are we going to do about our little situation we have here?" Strawberry asked as she sat back down. Frustrated by her intense hunger pains, that had began to beat up against her ribs, like an African drum.

"Well the way we see it, Tameia, we are now faced with two scenarios to choose from. Either we kill you, since you want to know too much or we allow you to join our elite group of women, seated right before your eyes," Nicole recited as she stood up, placing her hand in the soft smooth hair of Tameia.

"Wait a minute, so your telling me that you girls would kill me, rather than let me in what it is that your into?" She asked as she began to slowly back up out of the door, with her eyes still trained in on the females in front of her. Not realizing that Entyce was already a step ahead of her, standing behind her in the doorway of the pool house.

"Yes, she's absolutely correct." Entyce spoke up as Tameia quickly turned around to see her standing there. She was now surrounded inside the small pool house.

"So, what makes you think that we have something more sinister going on here?" Mignon asked as Tameia turned her small body frame around.

"I've known that something was up, a long time ago. I just didn't want to say anything. After I saw the way Michael and his lady friend looked the day I told you all about the witness over in Daytona. My questions were all answered then. So, are you girls going to let me in or what?"

"You sure you want to be involved with what we have going on?"

"Yes, Mignon. The way I see it, hell, I'm already involved. I stay here with you ladies right?"

"Yes you do, but you have never encountered nothing like what we have been involved with."

"You might be right, Nicole, but I know so much. So that makes me an accomplice, especially with the way the court system and I see it."

"She's right, Nicole."

"Thank you Strawberry!" Nicole replied with a smirk. "No problem, now let's get things in motion." The ladies all gazed at Strawberry, then looking back at Tameia, before actually telling her about what it was she wanted to get into.

Chapter 15
Tattoo!

Two full hours had went by inside that pool house as the ladies all explained their individual roles as a Murder Queen. During this time, Tameia listened with open eyes and ears highly tuned in, on how they were able to go under the radar, without being caught.

"So, let me get this straight. Not only are you ladies some fly ass female strippers that strip on the weekend and at Bachelor parties, but some hired killers as well?"

"Yes," Mignon answered with a serious unit on her face, voice remaining just as calm as a running river.

"You wanted to know right?" Nicole asked, eyes glued in on the pristine beauty.

"Yes Nicole," Tameia answered as she choked up, then swallowed the lump in her throat. "Okay, so now you have no choice but to join or take a bullet to the back of your head," Nicole uttered calmly as well as she looked over to Entyce, who actually had her hand nestled on her snub nosed forty five, chrome pistol. Tameia being unsuspected of the deadly intention's Entyce had planned for her, if she had a sudden change of heart.

Lil Tameia was calm as a fucking cucumber as she stated, now her eyes trained on them. "Like I said, the way I see it, I'm already a part of the elite group of women, known as The Murder Queens! Now, where do I sign up at?" She asked as she cut an evil grin at her partners in crime.

"This weekend, while we're all up in Duval county, remind us to take you to get a tattoo, just like the one we all have right here!" Mignon voiced as she slid up her skirt, revealing her tattoo, right next to her mouth watering pussy.

"Oh shit! Let me see that!" Tameia barked as she stood to get a better look at the tat. "Let me see too!" Strawberry shouted, desperately trying to get a peek at what she desired to suck on more than my brother's dick.

"Girl, if you don't sit you Bulldiking ass the fuck down, I know something!" Mignon replied, while trying to keep Strawberry from getting too close to what I desired from time to time. Like I have been saying from jump. Mignon was one of the most beautiful women I had ever come in contact with. And it was a damn shame, she never once allowed me that chance opportunity to have her in my bed, like most of the women during my tenure as the manager of the Florida Hot Girl's allowed me.

So while shaking my head up and down, seated at this typewriter, writing this book, if your reading this Mignon, you and a few top notch females that have been in my group. Just know, you were one of them that got away. Causing me to still have wet dreams about your fine red ass ...

When Mignon let Strawberry know how she felt, her feelings were deeply bruised as she uttered. "Don't worry, you fine piece of meat, keep playing with ole Berry and I'm come take something round here!"

"Yeah, like an ass whipping if you keep trying me," Mignon versed as she slid her skirt back down. "About that tattoo Mignon, we might have to think that one over."

"Why, what's wrong Nicole?" Tameia asked as she sat back down, disappointment written all over her face.

"Mignon, with the few bodies we have already left in Jacksonville, getting a tat there would definitely give ourselves up!"

"She's right Mignon, she's going to have to go to the same place we got ours done at, if we want to keep our identity a secret."

"You're right, Entyce. I didn't think about that. I tell you what, we still have enough time before we have to leave for tonight. So we all go to the mall together, so she can get tatted."

"And do some shopping too, right?"

"Yes Strawberry, anything else?" Nicole asked as she started laughing at her good friend.

"Matter of fact there is. I got shotgun, because I can't wait to ride in that new white Benz parked outside!"

"Whatever Strawberry. One more thing ladies."

"What's that, sis?" Nicole asked as she stopped in the doorway of the pool house. "What do we do about Reese?"

"We do what we always do, we kill his snitching ass!" Entyce muttered as the girls all went for the door.

"Hey, wait a minute?" Strawberry yelled as they all stopped dead in their tracks.

"What now Strawberry, damn!" Mignon asked as she blew steam out of her mouth. "What about Mike, do we call him and let him know what's going on?" The girls all looked amongst one another, before Mignon uttered.

"If I know Mike, he probably already knows. But what he doesn't know, won't hurt him. Now let's get ready and get to the mall, we still have to pick up that lil female Mo Money, and the rest of the crew. You all know how bad traffic is on a Friday night…

***

That night at dinner with the family, was when Firstborn and I finally met the rest of Rhynyia's high powered family of complicated business men in their countries drug trade. Her uncles and grandfather were all present at the dinner, sitting amongst the rest of the family, eating their meal right before they buried their loved one. Now my brother and I had already met her cool ass Uncle Felix. The one who I suspected might have killed her grandfather on her mother's side. But it was her Uncle Lorenzo, that at first glance looked just like someone I had seen before. Where, I just couldn't place my finger on where it was, but I was certain that I had seen his face before.

We all sat there eating as Firstborn and myself listened to which one of the family members talking amongst themselves about what had transpired during the days coming up to the funeral. As I sat there trying to eat, I couldn't help but feel the constant stare from Rhynyia's short pale faced grandfather. Especially with the way he cut his beady, little shifty eyes at me from time to time. I knew right then that it would only be a matter of time before he asked me questions about his lovely granddaughter and I just didn't know when it would be.

Rhynyia felt the glare from her grandfather as well as I did. All while seated next to me trying to concentrate on eating her food. She had to, since she was pregnant with child. I could sense the tension in the air and leaned over to her and quietly asked. "Hey, are you okay, beautiful?"

She dimly looked back over at me and whispered. "Yes Michael, I'm just thinking about the conversation I had earlier with Senor' Chulo."

"I understand, if it's anything that I can help you with, just let me know," I said to her as I cut off a nice piece of my juicy, tender steak that we were having for dinner.

As she went back to nibbling on her vegetable I guess everyone could sense by the way she was carrying herself that something was bothering her, they just didn't know what it was at the time.

My jug headed brother was seated right next to Pierre, who at first sight I thought that the both of them were talking about the funeral for Prince Naheed. That was until his lovely wife interrupted them both with.

"Pierre, do not talk of the family business at the dinner table, please."

He looked over to her and then said. "I'm so sorry my darling, you are positively correct. Where are my manners at tonight? He then lifted his glass of wine, smiling and tipping, as he slowly sipped the nice tasting beverage. Everything had went back to normal after he had sat his glass back down and continued eating. At least that's what I thought, until Rhynyia nudged my knee and whispered. "My stepmother just told my father not to talk about business at the table. What kind of business does my father and your brother have to talk about?"

I shrugged my shoulders and shook my head, then uttered. "I don't know, but I'm pretty sure we'll both know by the time we are to go back to Orlando."

"Ummh, huh," she said, then drank some of her water, all while glaring down at Firstborn, who sat at the table, like his ass was a fucking king or something. Then it dawned on me as I watched his ass, laughing and talking. Come to think about it, him and Pierre didn't even have anything in common, so why was he and Pierre so close now? Then I thought about it, he did say to me that once we got back, he was going to go back to Madison. My eyebrows frowned as I tried to read his lips, my attention was so focused on my brother, that I never heard her grandfather ask me. "So Michael, what are your plans for Rhynyia's future?" This is when she nudged me again, snapping me back to reality.

"My grandfather just asked you a question.

"I'm sorry sir, what was that again?" I asked.

"I said, what are your plans for Rhynyia's future?" I had to think quickly on my feet, so that he couldn't catch me slipping with a barrage of silly ass questions. So, I answered back with. "First sir." I paused as I wiped my mouth with my table napkin, then said. "I plan to marry her before the birth of our first child. And then." He then rudely cut me off in mid sentence, right before I was about to tell him of my other plans with a different tone in his voice.

"And what, let her continue dancing in the Go-Go strip clubs, shaking her ass for every man to see!" Everyone at the table immediately dropped their forks and sat still, waiting for me to answer. This is when the cool in me took over, I coyly laid back in my chair, thinking of what to say, when I happened to stare down at my rock headed brother, who was sitting there with the dumbest look on his face that I had ever seen. His demeanor caught me off guard for just a mere second, in which was just enough time to place her hand over my hand and said to me. "Let me handle this one baby…

Chapter 16
Shake her Ass!

Without haste, Rhynyia pushed her dining room chair back from the table and stared at her short, fat ass grandfather directly in his cold, shifty beady eyes. Right before saying. "I only dance when I desire too. Michael has and will never ask me to shake my ass in any gotdamn strip club. I do it because that is what I choose to do!"

He glared back at his granddaughter as if he wanted to choke on his half cooked steak. It damn near looked as if the man's face was turning a light pink as he sat there trying to cut into his rare, cooked steak. No one, not even him addressed the elephant in the room. Then without notice, she continued to rant with, "Or would you like for me to sell drugs to other parts of the world, like my father and grandfather before him?"

Leaping up from his chair, her father shouted. "Rhynyia!" His fork slammed to his half empty plate with force and anger.

She stood her ground as she dared to stare her father down as if she would've had a gun in her hand, she would've shot him right in front of the entire close knit family, herself. "Father, he came at my Michael the wrong fucking way! There is no damn way that I'm going to sit here and allow him to belittle the man that I love with all of my heart!" She had tears forming in the well of her eyes as she stood there, defending me. Hell, I was so caught off guard that I had tears of my own forming in my eyes as well. Hot tears to be exact.

"So you love this man more than you love this family?" Her father asked as he stood there.

"The man that sits next to me is my fucking family!" She growled back.

"I see," he replied as he sat back down, then looking amongst his brothers and father. Her grandfather then slowly bowed his head in shame, then looking over at his son, he whispered.

"She's right, Pierre, I had no right to say what I just said. I'm so sorry, Mr. Michael and to you as well my dear child. Please accept my deepest apologies." I slowly looked around the table as it seemed as though everyone was waiting for me to say something.

This is when I took my time, gathered my thoughts and uttered. "No problem, sir, I accept your kind apology."

He nodded his head and went back to cutting his rare steak. But my gorgeous bride-to-be had other plans.

"If you all don't mind, I would like to be excused from my meal and this dinner table."

"Go ahead, my child," her stepmother said as she sat there, stoned face. I tried to reach out for Rhynyia's hand, but she looked at me with pleading eyes. "No Michael, I'm good," she said as she moved my hand away. She was hurt and I knew it, just as much as I could see it.

When she was almost out of the room, the youngest person at the table, her little sister Maylia, looked at everyone at the table and articulated. "We can't have the family at odds during a time like this! Must I remind you all that we bury our dear brother, your son," she said as she looked at her father. "Your first grandson." She then looked at her grandfather. "Tomorrow and we're here at odds with one another, over nothing," she said with tears of her own, snaking down her cute, little splendid looking face. The young girl was so beautiful that I knew right then, that one day she would break some man's heart.

Pierre seen this and once again stood to his feet and apologized for the untimely outburst. After about ten more minutes of him talking, everyone agreed as we all left the dining room table, headed into the large foyer. I on the other hand excused myself and went upstairs to check on my picturesque looking Rhynyia. When I found her, she was spread across her massive bed, looking at pictures of her and her brother when they were both young kids. I didn't know what to say as I stood there looking down at her in bed, so I gently placed my hand on her neck and started massaging her neck. While she glared at one particular picture of the two of them together.

"So that's your brother, huh?" I asked as I slowly worked my way around her tender looking ass. Her eyes still held a few tears as she looked back at me and whispered.

"Yes Michael, the only one of my siblings that really understood me. I miss him so much. If I would have known that the last time I saw him was going to be the very last time I would ever see him, I would have never left Puerto Rico, in search of a mother who doesn't even want her own daughter."

By now her praline eyes could no longer hold back her tears that were trying to escape from the wells of her eyes. This is when she laid in my arms and then started sobbing, softly. I will be the first to admit at this time is when I felt like a straight piece of shit. For one, I knew her mother and I felt her pain. But one thing I have never felt before, was not having the love of my very own mother. Me and my sister grew up with both parents and there was no way that I knew how it felt to be without one. Even as a young child my father became ill and was away from us for a while. My dear mother filled that void for both parents.

So at that moment, I didn't know how to feel, but her pain did transfer over to my breaking heart all due to me knowing the very truth about her mother's unique situation and what was actually keeping them away...

As I sat there holding her, it became more painful to me as I sat there holding her, while she cried in my arms. I didn't know if I should tell her who her mother was or tell her what her father had said to me earlier. So confused and hurt, I simply said to her, "I'm pretty sure your brother is up in heaven, missing you too, Rhynyia."

"Yeah, if there is a heaven," she voiced in between her sobbing.

"What is that supposed to mean young lady?" I asked with a puzzled look on my face.

She then looked at me, while wiping her hot tears on my shirt. "With all the senseless killing and deaths around us, how could there be one?"

I gently pushed her away, looking her in her face. "Believe me young lady, there is a heaven, just as well as a hell. Let's just hope and pray that we both end up in the right place."

She then smiled at me as she pulled out a scrapbook of some old pictures.

"What's that?" I asked.

"Nothing, just an old scrapbook," she replied as she placed the book on her bed and began rumbling through the book.

Moments had passed, when she came across another picture that looked familiar. She then looked up at me and said. "This is the only picture that I have of my mother and I, together." When she passed the picture to me, I could see why Pierre had fell in love with her. It was a picture of a beautiful young woman who couldn't be no older than twenty one at the time. At first I thought that the young lady in the picture was none other than Rhynyia's sister. That was until I looked a little closer and realized that it was a younger version of Rhynyia's mother instead. I was petrified as the striking resemblance of Rhynyia and her mother stood out in the picture. They could have went for identical twins as much as they looked so much alike. Rhynyia then whispered something to me that snapped me back to reality. "I wonder why she never came back for me. Was she ashamed of me or did I do something so wrong that kept her from wanting to have me with her?"

"I don't know Rhynyia, but I'm pretty sure whatever the reason, she had a good one."

"So Michael, do you think that if I can get you the picture from my Uncle Felix, that you might be able to find her?"

I didn't want to look her in the eyes and lie to her, so I turned my head and said. "I'll do my very best to find her. I promise."

"Thank you. I love you so much. Thank the man upstairs for allowing you into my confused life," she said as her head fell back into my chest. Leaving me sitting there, knowing the truth about who her mother was and where she was. But deep down inside my soul, I believe that it might be her father, who didn't want her to find her mother. Hell, at that moment in time, I even felt like Pierre and her Uncle Felix had something to do with her grandfather dying in that car crash as well. I might not have known the truth about everything right then, but you can best believe that I was going to try my best to find the answers for her. At least I had one of the most dire questions for my girl, already tucked away inside of my head…

Chapter 17

Her Chest!

As I laid there with my brain going a mile a minute, my phone startled me as it vibrated inside of my slacks. I quickly pulled it out of my pocket and saw that it was none other than.

"Hello, Mignon."

"Hello to you as well Mike, how's your vacation?" She asked, sounding chipper and bright.

"I wish that it was a vacation, Mignon," I uttered as Rhynyia began to stir.

"My bad Mike, I'm just calling to let you know that we're about to head up to Jacksonville for the weekend."

"Cool, is everyone already with you?"

"No, not yet. We're about to go pick them up right now, on our way out."

"Sounds good, seems like you have everything under control."

"Yes, that I do. And oh, by the way, we picked up the truck earlier today and your boy Jeff said that they want to do another show in about two weeks."

"Good. So, who's with you right now?"

"Me, Nicole, Entyce and your girl Strawberry. And oh, the little, short girl, Tameia."

"Really, so how is Nicole doing?" I asked as Rhynyia turned up her lips, staring at me. "She's fine Mike, just a lil sore. Other than that, she's good."

"Okay, sounds good. We should be home on Monday night."

"No problem, how is my favorite girl, Rhynyia holding up?"

"She's okay. She's lying here on my chest as we speak. Do you want to speak to her?"

"Hell yeah, let me holla at my girl," she said while sounding all excited to speak with Rhynyia.

"Here, Mignon wants to speak to you." I said as I handed her the phone. Once the phone was in her hand, for some odd reason I wanted to use the restroom, so I went off to my room instead of using her's.

While walking down the hallway to my room, I happened to notice Firstborn's door to his room, slightly ajar. The closer I got to the door, I could faintly hear some familiar noises coming from behind the door. The noises piqued my curiosity so I peeked my head inside the door to witness him pushing his erect manhood deep inside of Rhynyia's sister's kidneys. The brother was going so deep inside of her, where no man had ever went before. Due to her still being a virgin all of her natural born life, the poor girl's knees were all the way up by her temple, with my gotdamn brother looking like he was actually standing up inside of the girl's pussy. She was taking his manhood like it wasn't hurting her at all, while he was attempting to write his full name inside of her fine, sexy ass. Now I know I had to be standing there for at least five or maybe ten minutes, before I had to take off for my room. The nice sexual moan she made drove me crazy.

"Uhhhh, Papi, you love me and me pussy?" She asked.

"You damn right I do! I love this pussy!" My foolish brother yelped as he straight punished the young virgin.

His back was facing me, so he couldn't see me standing there, but she could as she looked at me and winked with her right eye, then smiling, devilishly.

The entire time that I was standing there watching those two, I had forgot about using the bathroom. Just as I got inside of my bathroom I went to pull my slacks down and realized that my manhood had stiffened up, due to me watching how my brother was fucking the shit out of Rhynyia's sister. I then asked myself while washing my hands. *Should I go back inside Rhynyia's room and start making sweet, passionate love to her, or just left my manhood die down.*

After a few seconds, my decision was made up for me, when Rhynyia ran into my room with my phone in her hand, yelling. "Michael!"

I quickly turned around with my wash cloth in my hand, thinking what that she had caught my brother fucking her sister.

"Yeah, what's up?" I said with a stupid look on my face. I had to, this was my only way of acting like I didn't know what he was in there doing. But she surprised me when she said, "Telephone! I think it's your other baby mama!"

Damn, Sharon had called me right in the middle of Rhynyia talking with Mignon. I abruptly reached for my phone, while she stood there ear hustling, with her arms folded across her chest...

***

I could only imagine how her expression on her face looked as she waited for me to answer my phone. So as I took the phone, I knew how my expression looked. Let me tell you, it looked jacked the fuck up! Not only was my facial expression fucked up, but I was nervous as a Kentucky Chicken, with Colonel Sanders standing right there with some hot frying grease. Yeah, I was that nervous. So nervous that my mild meager voice trembled when I answered, sounding like my Pops, Buck Vallentino.

"Hellllo!"

Sharon cut right into my ass, like I cut into that juicy ass steak that I had ate earlier that night.

"So you just take your black ass over to Puerto Rico and don't even call back to check on my ass! You don't know if I was dead or still at that damn hospital y'all took my ass too!" She angrily barked into the phone, all the while with me standing there with what my mother called, the Sad Face. Good ole, Ethel Lou, always had a way with her words.

"It wasn't like that Sharon, you were still at the hospital and I didn't want to disturb you," I meekly replied, not trying not to show too much emotions, with Rhynyia standing right there, staring into my face.

"Fuck that, Michael Vallentino. I'm carrying your fucking child, so you could have at least came by the hospital to see about me and your child!"

"I did, but it was so much commotion going on at the hospital that I didn't want to stay."

"What the fuck ever, Michael. So, you could at least gave me a call."

"Your right, my bad. I promise to call you as soon as I get back to Orlando," I said with a slight sigh.

"Okay, I'll believe that shit, when your black ass gets back into town."

"For real, Sharon, I promise. Now how are you and the baby doing?" I asked, with Rhynyia in the background mumbling. *'I promise Sharon!'*

I pointed at her with my index finger. "Shut up!"

"The baby and I are doing just fine," she muttered as she continued short, right to the point answers.

"So how is everything else in Orlando?" I asked, trying to keep her from asking me any personal questions. "I guess you haven't heard the news about one of those officers who helped kidnap me and Bre, did you?"

"No, the last thing I heard was that they were all shot up pretty bad."

"Well, I guess I'll go ahead and tell you what happened to one of them. Somebody got to the one officer named John Hatfield while his ass was supposed to be heavily guarded by the same police department who allowed their officers to kidnap my ass."

"What?" I asked as I took a seat on the edge of the bed, looking back up at Rhynyia, who seemed like she wanted to know just as much as I did.

"Yes, somebody killed him," Sharon said to me while Rhynyia was trying to ask me what happened. I swiftly placed my index finger up to my mouth. Telling her to hold on, but she wouldn't stop. So I placed my hand over the phone and told her. "She said that someone killed one of the officers that had kidnapped her."

"Oh shit!" Rhynyia yelled while standing there, staring me directly in the face. "So, what killed him?"

I asked, trying to keep her mind off of me and her relationship. "I have no idea. They released me the very next day."

"Well as long as you are alright, that's all that matters."

"I guess. Hey, I know that your so-called girlfriend is standing there looking in your mouth, so just call me when you have some free time."

"Okay, I'll do that Sharon." Rhynyia then did the unthinkable when she yelled through the phone with,

"Hey Sharon, I'm glad that you and the kids are safe and sound!"

"What did she say Michael?"

"She said hello and that she's glad that you and the kids are safe and sound. You know it was her who wanted to be there and help rescue you from the crooked ass cops?"

"For real?" She asked, with a bit of sarcasm laced inside of her voice.

"Yes, she was the one who actually put up the ransom money for your rescue."

"Mike, are you serious?" She asked, trying to make me believe that she really cared. "Yes Sharon, she has no ill feelings towards you. She really likes you, if you ask me."

"Whatever, Mike. by the way, since we're talking about the rescue. Who was that chick seated in the back seat, with my head laying in her lap? I had my head turned to the side and I really couldn't get a good look at her. But her face looked real familiar to me?"

Chapter 18
Without A Paddle!

Here I was again, stuck somewhere without a muthafucking paddle or answer. Sharon had me stuck right there like a fucking deer in headlights. What was I to do now? How could I tell this smart ass female that the person's lap was none other than the same fucking female, who helped my brother and I get rid of her fat, stank ass Uncle Bernard "Fats" Walker. I was just about to say that the female had been killed right after that night, but I guess this is when my girl seen the astonishment covering my bewildered looking face. Because she speedily snatched the phone from me.

"Hello, Sharon," Rhynyia spoke into the phone as the two of them started talking to one another, with me on the other hand, stepping outside of her room, walking back down the hallway to witness Natasha stumbling out of my brother's room, half naked and dripping of her own sweat.

His foolish black hearted ass was standing there in the doorway of his room, with nothing but a towel draped around his waist. Natasha paused for a brief moment, I guess she was trying to gain her balance. Once she had it, her hot booty ass stood on her tiptoes, so she could give my brother a kiss on his cheek.

When the sneaky, lil fast ass hussy saw me standing there, mouth agape, she winked at me again with her right eye. Right after that she gave me a wicked ass smile, without

Firstborn noticing that I was even behind them, watching everything. This is when I quickly turned around to walk back into my room, when I heard Rhynyia coming my way, yelling out.

"Michael!" I had to hurry up and get out of sight. There was no way in hell, that I was going to let her find out that my thick headed ass brother was fucking the shit out of her sister.

"Yes baby girl," I said as I made it into my room, when I turned to see her, she was trying to hand me back my phone. I guess she didn't catch her nasty ass sister leaving my brother's room. "You just forgot about poor ole Mignon, on the other line, didn't you?" I asked her as her face now held a warm smile on it. "Nah, she had hung up when I told her that Sharon was calling on the other line."

"Oh."

"You know your girl is pretty cool."

"Who?"

"Sharon! Oh, silly ass man," she said with a side smirk.

"What are you talking about now, Rhynyia?"

"Sharon, Michael. I think when I do come back home, me and her should really get together and hang out. You know, bond together some how. We both are having your child you know?" She said, but when I heard what she had said at first, I knew that my little secret was about to be exposed way sooner than I wanted it too. My dire situation now was, how in the hell was I going to be able to keep it a secret any longer? First there was Pierre, who wanted to find her mother before Rhynyia did. Then, there was Rhynyia who wanted to find her as soon as she could. Then, there was my black ass, who knew the awful truth already. There was no way that I could let those two women become close friends, not right now, not ever if I wanted to have the both of them in my confused and complicated life. Now I was going to have to utilize every avenue I could, to keep the two of them from finding out the truth. But first I was going to have to talk to the one person who was keeping everything a secret as well as I was.

Who knew, maybe it was something that she wanted to keep from them, forever. Whatever the reason, I wasn't about to expose the secret until everyone was ready. And besides, I had way bigger problems on my head to contend with. And I wasn't about to get another problem started, not right then and damn sure not at that moment. I just couldn't and to believe it all, that was just at the juncture in my life. Who knew that right down the road, my ever growing empire was about to crumble, right before my very eyes. My dumb ass just couldn't see it. If I would have, I would have never, ever moved back home, to Lakeland, Florida. Why, because like I just said, this is where my life as the manager of the world famous Florida Hot Girls, would come to an abrupt halt, all due to a fucking Rat, who I would meet some years later, while doing talent shows for my entertainment group called, Big Boy Entertainment Group …

***

That night I was tossing and turning as I laid there half naked in the vast bed, that was fit for a king, such as myself. At least that's what I wanted to believe. I wasn't alone though, because dancing inside my head were the thoughts of the beautiful Sharon Conoly, along with the dreadful secrets that were embedded inside my head for safe keeping. When I did finally manage to fall asleep, Rhynyia found her way into my bedroom, claiming that she would rather sleep with me, rather than her colossal, colonial style bed.

I didn't mind, due to us leaving in the next few days, so I welcomed her presence alongside me once again.

Not even caring if her father found us together, hell she was practically my wife already. So that was the last thing on my mind.

"You don't mind do you?" She asked as she let her robe fall to the floor. Now, she stood there in the midnight moon, covered in her nice Julio London lingerie. Her body was flawless as I laid there gazing at her. "Hell nah, hold up for just one minute," I said to her as I searched for my phone.

"What are you doing, silly man?" She asked, half a smile on her lovely face.

"My phone, I need to play this one particular song by my boy, Prince."

"What song is that, bae?"

Once I found my phone I scrolled down to the right song and hit the play button. Just as I did that is when I slowly turned my head around and began singing right along with my man. The song was one of his classic hit slow songs. The title was none other than *Insatiable*. And that's exactly how she looked at me that night, with the moon glaring through her beautiful black hair.

"I love this song."

"I know you do, you should. You look just like the woman he is describing in the song."

She playfully hit me in the arm as she spoke. "Whatever boy! Now come over here and make sweet, passionate love to your baby mama!"

"Say less, my Princess." Was all I said as I climbed on top of her. I guess she had been wanting to make love to me all night, because my stiff manhood slid right inside of her wetness and warmth. "Damn, my pussy is so tight!" I said to her as I felt my wood hit the bottom of her stomach.

"What, it wasn't supposed to be tight or something?" She asked as she bit my ear lobe.

"Nothing Rhynyia, it's just me enjoying how the way your pussy feels wrapped tight around my dick."

"Shut up and fuck me like you missed me." Was all she said as I placed her legs up over my shoulders and went for broke.

"Ummmm, just like that Michael. Tear your pussy up, bae!"

"You don't have to tell me twice." I uttered as I took control and made love to her fine ass for almost a full hour. We were both so tired and worn out that she dozed off, immediately after I pulled out. Leaving me awake, worrying about the safety and well being of my precious Florida Hot Girls. All alone, dancing back in Jacksonville, Florida. Maybe, just maybe if they all would have had one inclination of the trouble that lay ahead for them, they might not have ventured up there on this particular weekend. I knew they were in Jacksonville, but were they okay and were they making money, doing what they did best? After briefly speaking with Mignon, all I could hope for now, was the mere fact of them being okay and out of harm's way.

Now like I told you before, I really never like leaving the girls alone, to fend for themselves. Hell, I really never liked the idea of them leaving with a guy after a show, if that guy wasn't me or whoever I had hired to watch over them. It was a way I felt the entire time I worked with any of the Florida Hot Girls, from Orlando, to Tampa, to Daytona Beach, even the ones I had when I went to live in Gainesville with this one chick, who later on down the line broke my heart into tiny little pieces. Don't worry, you'll get to know her, sooner than later. She knows who she is and what she did to me and my heart. Let's just say that her initials are L.W.

Now back to the story. I was so worried about the girls and their safety, that I rolled out of bed and sat at the edge of it, pondering over what they were doing? I was so caught up with worry and pain that I had told myself that as soon as the funeral was over, my brother and I would have to get back home, so that I could keep a watchful eye over my over growing empire of beautiful, tantalizing, exotic women, that were known to the world as the world famous Florida Hot Girls…

***

Meanwhile, the entire crew of women in the ever growing stable were all inside dancing at Black Magic when Lil Kitty found Mignon over at the bar, counting up her money.

"Excuse me Mignon, since Mike placed you in charge of the group, while he's gone, I guess I should be asking you."

Mignon dully turned away from counting her large stash of cash and asked. "And what is it that you have to ask me, Lil Kitty?"

"Oh, it's really not much, but I might be leaving the club tonight with my lil boo thang, Punkin. Is that okay with you?"

"Oh really?" Mignon asked as her face turned upside down, just hearing the guy's name through the stale air of the already crowded club.

"Yeah, if that's alright with you?" Lil Kitty asked, not knowing what to expect from the new boss in charge. Mignon now gave her full attention to Lil Ms. Hot Ass. Even inhaling some of the stale air inside the club, then blowing it out.

"Listen Lil Kitty, I might need for you to fall back when it comes to that lil ass nigga, Punkin. You see I really believe that him and his crew, maybe looking for some get back. Especially with the way they found some of their homies last weekend."

"Oh really, that was kind of fucked up, how the po-po's found them boy's last weekend, wasn't it?" Lil Kitty said as she looked at Mignon with pure concern and doubt written all over her face.

"Yeah and for some odd, strange reason Kitty, I just don't trust his lil trifling ass. So just hold on and let me check things out before you or any of the girls make any moves. Besides, you know how Mike would have a fit if anything happened to his precious, Lil Kitty!" She just had to pump up her already big head. Once Lil Kitty heard that a great big smile erupted onto her cute lil face as she looked at Mignon and said.

"Whatever Mignon. You think he feels like that about lil ole me?"

"Yes Kitty, I know Mike is beating the brakes off of your lil hot ass!"

I don't know how she knew, but how right her ass was about that …

Chapter 19
Walking and Stumbling!

Lil Kitty was still smiling as Mignon lazily turned back around and continued counting up her loot. She had just erased her little devilish smile away when she tried to ask Mignon.

"So, who do you think it was who took them clowns out last weekend?"

"I have no idea Kitty, but whoever it was who did it, did your girl Chyna a real big favor, didn't they?" Mignon asked her as she stood up from the bar, adjusting her outfit that seemed to be cutting up between her two thick ass pussy lips.

"Yes, that they did," Lil Kitty responded back to her, while having her signature smile over her cute little face.

"Go ahead and finish making your money, I'll get with you before we all get ready to leave the club."

"Okay, thanks, Mignon."

"Don't mention it," Mignon replied as she stood there watching as Lil Kitty walked her small frame ass across the room, with her thin ass thong, sideway's up in the crack of her narrow ass.

Just as Lil Kitty walked out of eye sight, Richard eased up to the bar with a blunt, dangling from his dry, crusty ass lips.

"I really don't trust that nigga Lil Kitty wants to leave with after the club," Mignon uttered as Richard desperately tried to maintain his balance on the bar stool.

"Who? The one they call Punkin?" he asked while blowing out the smoke from the Loud nice ass weed that he was smoking on.

"Yes, for some reason, I just have this funny feeling about him and the crew of niggas that he hangs out with. I still don't think that they have learned their lesson after the last time we had to deal with them."

Oh, that is the lil dude that was with them boys who ran a train on my girl Strawberry, wasn't it?" He asked as he sat there, gazing over at the guy, who he couldn't really see that well, since the weed was fucking with his eyes sight.

"Yes, Richard." She answered with a smirk on her face. "And if you ask me, they still might have some animosity towards us for the way Mike handled their ass," she voiced.

"Not to mention with the way I acted also," Richard said as he flexed his shoulder, trying to make a muscle. Mignon couldn't help but to look down at his small ass arm and said.

"Yeah right, Richard. You did do your part." Her lips curled as she stared at the man, knowing damn well was all he did was to just stand there, watching what I was doing the entire time.

"Mignon, he's harmless, girl. You worry too much, just let the shit ride. Everything will be okay, you starting to act just like Mike now," he managed to say as he began beating his chest real hard, due to him inhaling too much of the weed at one time.

After a few minutes of him coughing so hard that he had some type of greenish phlegm, that he had nowhere to wipe it on. Mignon saw the greenish mess all over his hand and shouted out.

"Ewww, that's fucking gross, Richard, here, boy. Take this napkin and wipe that shit off of your hand!" Richard quickly took the napkin and began wiping his hand. "Boy you really need to stop smoking if that shit is causing your ass to cough up shit like that, on your fucking hand!"

"Nah, this is just some good ass fucking weed!" He replied as his drunk ass stumbled away from the bar, trying to make it to the restroom.

'I wonder what in the hell did Chazz put in this blunt?' He mumbled to himself as he continued coughing, violently as he walked through the large crowd of people, even bumping into a few patrons on his way to the restroom, before he pissed all over himself.

"Yeah, try that shit, Richard!" Mignon yelled out, as she stood there laughing at the way he was walking and stumbling. *'Boy, if Mike could see your black ass right now, your ass would be so fired!'* Mignon said to herself as she once again adjusted her outfit, then walking away from the bar, searching out for the Murder Queens…

While walking through the crowd of women and men, one of the patrons yelled out to Mignon.

"Hey Red, please let me get a dance over here!" The tall slim gentleman asked as she strolled. A nice big smile came across her face as she saw the nice stack of bills he had to throw at her in the background, you could hear the DJ announce throughout the club.

"Alright ladies and gentlemen, the Florida Hot Girls are in the building tonight, so make sure that you tip them well!" The crowds went wild as most of the tables had one or two, maybe even three of the Florida Hot Girls at their table doing their thang. The DJ had the club all hyped up, while playing the song, Shake What Ya Mama Gave You, by JT Money. The place was going hysterical, with money and thongs flying all through the stale air of the club.

The place was so much in a frenzy that none of the ladies even seen their adversary, Marquise walk into the small building, with malice and revenge on his mind. The large beast of a man had the obscured look of a wild mad man in his red colored eyes. Nothing could make him more happy but sweet revenge for the death of his younger brother and dear cousin. Not to mention the payback he craved for the death of his dear friend, Death Certificate. The pain and anguish he now suffered from, was damn near driving the man insane. He was so stricken with it, that the man had to be placed on all types of psychological pills, in order for him to just make it through the day. First, he had to take a pill in the morning, just as soon as he woke up. Then, another in the middle of the day. Last but not least, the poor sick son of a bitch, had to take one to make his big, nasty looking ass fall asleep. And to make matters worse, he now found himself clutching on to any bottle of cheap liquor he could find, just to drown out the hideous sight of the way his brother and close friend were found. He had even felt bad that in the end, Rasheed didn't want to kill the one lone girl he was sent to get rid of. Funny thing about that though, is that that one lone female, didn't feel any remorse for killing him.

But as soon as he witnessed Nicole from across the smoke-filled room, he could see why it was so hard for Rasheed to do the deadly deed.

'Damn, that lil short bitch is all that!' Marquise mumbled as he took a table in the back of the club.

"Would you like anything to drink, sir?" The young waitress asked him as he snapped back from La-La Land.

"Yeah, let a nigga get one of them Corona's and hey."

"Yes, sir." She answered as her head quickly snapped around to stare at the ugly guy.

"Don't put that fucking lime or lemon in my gotdamn drink!" He snarled as the waitress walked away, saying out loud. "Whatever, ole ugly ass nigga!"

Just as she had got out of sight, he pulled out fifth of Wild Irish Rose. He took the top off, then drank straight from the bottle, gulping the bottle as if it was water and he was dying of thirst. Now that he knew that Nicole and the rest of the Murder Queens had took out three of the most important people in his complicated life as though their miserable ass lives meant nothing to them. An act that he deemed to only be cold hearted and if they could kill his men and have no remorse or ill feelings towards them, so could he. He would have to just be more delicate in picking the right location, place and time to take them out.

Now while he sat his big black ass in the back of the club, the guy Mignon was dancing on, spoke something softly into her right ear. "You see that big, ugly ass nigga in the back of the club?"

"Who, the one that looks like a wild boar?" She asked, still maintaining her composure. "Yeah, the one that's sitting with the lil, short nigga Punkin."

"I see him."

"Well that's the one. He was the one who sent Rasheed your way. And the brother of them niggas who were killed last week," the guy stated.

"Oh yeah?" She asked, playing off her intentions.

"Yeah. By the way, you know the police still have no clues as to who actually did the dirty deed. If you ask me, I believe that it was just some angry females who had had enough of them nigga's shit," the guy spoke as she kept grinding on his stiff manhood. She was actually enjoying the way his wood felt up against her quite large pussy lips. "You don't say?"

"Yep," he replied.

"Well once I find out, you will be the first to know," she replied as she pushed her ass down hard onto his erect manhood. She was really into it now and if she was into fucking someone inside of a strip club for money, she might have taken him into the VIP room and fucked the shit out of his ass. But not this night and time. She had other important things on her mind. Besides, just as she had finished getting her information from the guy who kept her abreast of what transpired up in Duval county, she heard him let out a loud,

"Ahhhhhh, shiiiiiit!" Her head quickly snapped around.

"You okay?"

"Hell nah, your fine ass has made me cum all up inside my fucking clothes!" He whispered, embarrassed as to what had just taken place.

"Oh shit. You okay?" She asked as she eased up off of his lap.

"I'm good, your fine ass pushed down onto my dick and it felt as if I was actually fucking. Let me go clean this shit off. Thanks for the dance, Mignon," he said as she stood up. Then reaching for a stack of bills at the table.

"Nah, thank you for the dance and much needed info. See you soon, baby boy." She versed as she began picking up the stacks of money.

"Yeah and when you find out who has been whacking these niggas, please let me know," he said as he walked away from the table, ego fucked up. But him being relieved of a nut.

"Damn shame ole boy has that problem. If not, he might have been able to sample just how good this pussy really is," she said out loud, just as one of the girls walked up to her.

"Excuse me, big sis?"

"Yeah, what's good Nicole?" Mignon asked as she bent over and picked up the remainder of her money from dancing on the one guy who was her information guy, she had made at least four hundred dollars off his tall, lanky ass.

"I just seen Punkin and a few of his goons sit down at that table over there."

"I know, you see the one big, ugly, nasty looking guy?" She asked, pulling at her moist vagina.

"Yeah."

"Well that's the guy I believe is after the ones responsible for killing his people."

"Oh yeah?"

"Yes. Go ahead and continue dancing, while I go get myself cleaned up. When I get back, we will go over to their table and fuck with them for a minute or two."

"Yeah, okay. Go ahead and get yourself right, girl. Because it looks like you have just got through fucking."

"What?" Mignon asked.

"Yeah, either ole boy done bust a nut all over you and your costly ass outfit, or you have bust one on his ass." Nicole versed as she walked away laughing, leaving Mignon standing right there in her mess as well as the guy she had just danced on. Or should I say, nutted all over…

Chapter 20
Black and Mild!

Nicole walked away, looking for anyone that wanted a dance with her gorgeous ass. As I stated in the very beginning, she was not just gorgeous, but drop dead beautiful. Marquise knew it just as well as his eyes locked in on her.

"So, that's the one right there, huh?" He asked as he looked over at Punkin.

"Yes sir, that's the one they call Nicole," he replied. Meanwhile, Mignon was back in the dressing room. She had just finished cleaning herself off, now seated in front of the mirror, applying more make up to her already cute face. She took a deep sigh as she relished in her mind, that maybe she should just off Marquise right where his black ass was seated.

"Nah, can't do that. There's no way that I want the rest of the girls to suffer from my dire consequences." She thought out loud.

Most of all, she didn't want her actions to harm any innocent bystanders, nor cause a sheer disaster if she shot around all the people in attendance. So she had to think of another way, other than inside the club. Unbeknownst to her and her counterparts, Marquise was seated inside the booth, thinking the same as Mignon was. Now as she sat at the chair in the dressing room, deep in thought, Nicole didn't find anyone that attracted her enough to dance on, so she made her way into the dressing room.

"What's the plan, chick?" She asked Mignon.

Her head never even raised up as she simply replied. "It's complicated, Nicole. But did you get a good look at the guy?"

"Yes, him and a few of the other guys, now seated inside the booth with him. Matter of fact, the reason I'm back here is that I believe he knows that I'm the reason his boy got whacked.

"Hell, for all that it's worth, we all are," Mignon stated as she stood up, a new outfit adorned her curvaceous body as she stood and gave herself a look in the full length mirror. "So I guess he knew that we were all coming here for the weekend, huh?"

"I guess so, Nicole. Like I told you guys earlier in the week. If it wasn't for Lil Hot ass Kitty, we wouldn't even be here. Now all of us are in jeopardy."

"I know that's right. So I guess Punkin knew this all too well also, since he was the one who called her," Nicole spoke as both girls waltzed back outside the dressing room. They didn't want their conversation being heard by any loose ears.

"Yep, oh shit! Wait a minute!"

"What Mignon?" Nicole asked, alarmed by Mignon's loud outburst.

"Take a look for yourself." Nicole then took a closer look to witness Lil Kitty over at their booth. "Damn! Damn! Damn!"

"Yep and I told her ass to fall back from Punkin and now her lil ass is over inside their fucking booth. Now Mignon had to really think of something quick on her feet. "I'm 'bout to walk over there and tell her that you need to speak with her," Nicole said just as she was about to walk away. But she quickly stopped when she felt a sharp pain, where she had inadvertently shot herself in the chest. Now knowing if

Mignon noticed it, she would tell her ass to fall back to, so she played it off with. "Damn! I almost fell."

"Yeah, I seen that." Mignon uttered, just as a slim chick from Duval walked up beside them and asked.

"Hey, what are y'all looking at? If it's ole boy over there that looks like a wild boar, his black nasty ass has some very long paper," the lil slim chick said.

"Oh yeah?" They both asked in unison. "Yes ma'am. But he might be a bit sad, since he lost his brother, close friend and business partner last week."

"Oh yeah, what happened?" Mignon asked as she played stupid. "All I know is that they say it was a hit, by the Mafia! They say that the nigga over there be getting his coke from some made nigga. Well when he came up short with the money he owed, they cut off some of his workers' life support systems, if you know what I mean."

Both girls looked at one another, then back at the lil slim chick.

"For real?" Mignon asked, now really trying to play off her knowledge of what they both knew.

"Yeah, but if you ask me, I believe it was those bitches from down South!" The chick stated.

"Down South? What bitches are those?" Nicole spoke up.

"It's like this, they say that it's some bitches from down South that go around killing niggas for hire. They say them hoes are the fucking truth." Her eyes were wide open as she spoke.

"That bad, huh?" Nicole asked, a smirk on her face.

"Hell yeah! The police went on T.V. last week and said that the way them brothers were killed last week was some awful, foul shit. One niggas dick was stuck inside is partners ass, while his dick was shoved inside the other guys open mouth."

"Gotdamn!" Both females uttered in unison. The women were so busy talking, that they didn't even notice the bartender Jarvis over to the side of them.

It wasn't until he shouted. "Hey, who are you guys looking at?"

The lil slim chick quickly uttered. "I'm gone y'all, be safe."

"Peace," Mignon uttered, then looked over at Jarvis. "Nothing, young ass nigga. Just keep serving the drinks, with yo' young ass, before them eyes see something that it didn't want to see!" Nicole said while frowning up her face as the pain in her chest became more increasing to bear.

"I already saw what I wanted to see!" He barked while passing a customer a beer.

"And what might that have been young man?" Mignon asked as she placed her hand on her friend's back, about to ask her was she okay.

"That nice phat ass pussy of yours!" He replied, while smiling, showing off the lower part of his mouth, that he had adorned with gold teeth.

"Boy, shut your ass the fuck up!" Mignon quickly shouted as she sat next to her partner in crime.

They now had to hatch out a plan of attack. Meanwhile, Lil Kitty had just pulled Punkin away from the booth, saying to him. "Hey Punkin, about later tonight."

"Yeah, what's good, lil mama?" He asked, while rubbing his two hands together as if it was cold inside the small ass club.

"Something came up, so I don't think that I'll be able to leave with you tonight after the club."

"No problem, baby girl, there's always tomorrow," He said back to her, while smoking on his Black and Mild …

After Lil Kitty had finished conversion with Punkin, Nicole looked back over at Mignon and said.

"Alright Mignon, her lil naive ass is walking away, what do you want to do now?"

"Tonight isn't his night to die. We'll do this tomorrow night and then drive straight back to Orlando. In the meantime, grab Lil Kitty's dumb ass and have her to dress in with the rest of the ladies. It's time to get the fuck up out of here."

Mignon didn't feel quite right about that night. Especially with what the lil slim chick had just told the both of them. So she felt that time was of the essence.

"I'll be right back, chick," Nicole spoke as she gingerly walked away, still in a bit of pain.

Mignon then pulled Entyce over to her and whispered into her ear. "Have all of the ladies dress in and meet me at the truck."

"What about Richard's crew of girls?"

"His crew as well."

Richard was up at the stage area gazing up at the girls on stage. His block headed ass wasn't even aware of Marquise staring a hole right through the back of his large head.

"Hey Punkin, is that the nigga that be bringing those hoes up here?" Marquise asked as he leaned over to his right-hand man. Punkin dully turned around, slightly, trying to look over at the stage. When he seen that it wasn't his man, he turned back around and said.

"Nah, that's not his ass. His cool ass is a lil taller and a slight bit more buff than that lame ass dude. They do look somewhat alike though. Besides, the nigga that be bringing them up here is smoother than that cat right there!" He spoke loudly, due to the music being so loud inside of the club.

"Oh yeah?" Marquise said as he sipped slowly from the Corona bottle.

"Yeah, but he's the dude that walked in with them bitches." His black ass partner named Carlos, uttered.

"I know that shit, silly ass nigga! But he's not the nigga who runs the group." Punkin yelled at Carlos, while they all kept staring at Richard.

By now Mignon and Nicole could see that Marquise and his goons had their eyes glued on Richard.

"What do you want to do?" Nicole asked.

"Hold up, we good. Just as long as they don't make a move on Richard, we cool. If they do, we cut up!" Mignon replied.

"Gotcha!" Nicole uttered as she placed her hand on her four five. Back over at the booth, Marquise spoke up with.

"Well I don't care who his ass is. The problem we have now is that we can't do them hoes tonight!" He then fell back hard against the back of the booth.

"Why?" Flash asked as he looked eager to kill someone.

Because, ole stupid ass nigga! If we kill them hoe's tonight! The nigga who's actually in charge of them bitches is going to come back for revenge and probably shoot up the whole fucking town, while looking for us. We have to get that nigga right along with all of his hoes!"

"That might be a problem, Marquise."

"And why is that Punkin?"

"Because, like I said, his ass is in Puerto Rico with his bitch."

"Damn!" Marquise said as he slammed his fist down on the dirty, raggedy, beat-up old ass table, angrily. That's when Mignon walked her fine ass over by their booth and winked at Punkin, while smiling at Marquise. Chills went up the back of poor lil Punkin at that moment. He even almost pissed all over himself. Mignon was that one female, who put fear into most men's hearts, she was just that deadly…

At first thought, the huge, massive being of a man was caught completely off guard as the splendid looking Mignon spoke to him. For a moment there his ass thought that he was actually dreaming, as his mouth fell to his chin. How could such a beautiful woman be speaking to his not so attractive looking ass. "Is everything okay over here?"

"Yes, everything is fine, now that you have graced our booth with your presence," Marquise recited as he pushed stank breath Jimmy out of the way, so that she could sit next to him. "I was standing over there waiting for my friends to come out, when I happened to notice your fine chocolate looking ass over here at the booth, with your goons here," she sputtered as she took a good look at all of the goons seated inside the booth, making them feel comfortable with her being there. Marquise seen his chance at the gorgeous looking woman and quickly asked.

"Oh really, so what are you trying to get into on a beautiful, early Saturday morning?" Mouth smiling wide as he took out a nice fat sack of weed and promptly began rolling up a nice fat blunt.

"Shit, a girl like me is trying to see what them pockets be like!" She said as she nudged up under his huge, thick, sloppy ass arms that stretched along the seat of the booth.

"What's really good then? We can make this shit happen. Just say the magical word," he said as he smiled at his partners, then came right back with, "Do you smoke lil mama?" Just as the words rolled off of his chapped lips, he sparked up his blunt, still smiling at the young vixen, sitting up under him. From around the booth, without any notice at all, came the sultry voice of none other than my lil boo thang, Mo Money. Without Mignon knowing, I had spoke with her right before I left and told her to make sure the girls would be safe. For some reason, deep down, she just seemed like she would be a good fit with them Murder Queens.

"Nah, she doesn't, but I do." The goons at the booth all turned, stunned at what they were looking at, then yelling out in unison.

"Dammmmmmnnn and who in the fuck are you, beautiful?" As they all tried to make room for her as well. She placed her small hands on her lovely waist and said. 'Let me introduce myself, they call me Mo Money and the nice sexy ass bitch next to me is my girl, Entyce. And I'm pretty sure that you all know, Ms. Strawberry." They did. They were some of the same guys that had took her that night and had their way with her, for the free. Mo Money knew the story all too well. The goons all looked around at each other, wondering what to do next, even Marquise, who sat there speechless for a brief minute. As he thought to himself of what to do next. *'Do these bitches even know that I'm the nigga who's about to wack all of them?'* He said to himself.

Then his lil head, started thinking for his big head, with the senseless idea of fucking Mignon first, then the lil short light skin one that called herself, Mo Money.

"Damn, it looks like we have ourselves a full fucking house. I say we all go get some breakfast and then go from there," Marquise said as he pulled out a nice thick wad of cash. That's when the ladies inside the booth all looked around at each other with smiles on their faces. That's when Mo Money took charge of the situation and replied back with,

"We down with whatever is clever, my young black, thick brother!" The words slowly rolled off of her sexy ass lips as she uttered those sentiments, while looking directly at Marquise. Showing him the nice plate of gold teeth that she had just purchased at the Flea Market. Hands down, Jacksonville had the best Flea Markets in Florida.

"Let me make sure that my stable of ladies are okay and then we can all go from there. Better yet, just meet us outside in the parking lot," Mignon voiced as the ladies stood up from the booth.

"Sounds good to me, ma. Don't be playing either. I'm parked on the side of the building in a blue Ford Expedition, sitting up nicely on some twenty-four inch rims. The nicest truck on the block...

The four ladies were up and walking back towards the dressing room, when Mignon damn near tore Mo Money's arm off, then angrily asked her.

"Hey, what in the hell do you think you were doing back there?"

Mo Money quickly looked at the person who held her tightly by the arm. Her eyes told Mignon that she wasn't scared of her ass at all. "First of all, take that gotdamn paw off of my arm, before you lose it. Second of all, I was just following your lead, Mignon," she uttered as she snatched her arm away with attitude.

"What fucking lead and who in the hell do you think your talking to with that bass in your voice, little girl?" The two ladies were standing toe to toe, face to face, when Nicole stepped in between the both of them with, "Ladies, ladies, it's cool. Be easy, Mignon, I was the one who sent her."

"What?" Mignon asked as she swiftly turned her head in Nicole's direction.

"Yes. I sent her, besides she claims that Mike told her to stay close on our backs," she said, then looked at Mo Money.

"Go ahead and make sure everyone else is getting dressed, while I handle this."

Mo Money was ready to fight as she stood there, eyes focused on Mignon. Even though she might have been a bit younger than Mignon, Mo Money had spunk and a lot of fight, bottled up inside of her lil curvaceous frame. She could be a real fire cracker if tested by any of the females in the group. Lil Kitty would be the first one to find that out the hard way. Mo Money then cut a wicked smirk at Nicole and said, "Yeah, you handle that, before I have to."

"Alright lil girl, just because the nigga your ass is laying up with isn't here, doesn't make you any better. You better do as your told, before I snatch a plug out your lil hot ass! You got me twisted!" Mignon barked.

"Whatever," Mo Money said as she laughed, then turned on her heels and walked away, headed to the dressing room.

"Now, back to you Nicole. Why did you tell her lil grown ass to step in like that?"

Nicole took a deep breath, then she looked up in the face of her dear friend, before saying, "I saw you over at the nigga's booth and figured that you might need some help."

"Okay, so why didn't you step in?" Mignon asked as she turned, surveying who might be looking at the both of them talking.

"Well maybe I felt if I stepped in, somehow the big nigga would have realized that we were on to his ass."

"She does have a point there, Mignon," Entyce said as she stood side by side with Nicole.

"Damn! I didn't see it like that."

"We know, you were doing what you do best, Mignon."

Mignon then quickly turned to where that voice originated from. "And what does that supposed to mean Strawberry?"

"It means that your fine sexy ass always thinks faster on your feet. Which sometimes leaves the rest of us guessing."

Mignon then placed her hands on her hips, then saying, "My fault, ladies. You all do have a point. I guess I should apologize to ole girl, huh?"

"You think?" Nicole uttered.

"Yeah, you right." She then instructed the females with her on what to do as she walked away to collect the individual bar fees from the rest of the ladies. While she obtained the ladies tip out fees, she told them what time to meet up at the hotel for the meeting. Meanwhile, Nicole had made it back to the dressing room, to see Mo Money who was seated inside one of the chairs, lacing up her heels.

"Hey you?"

"Yeah."

"You okay?" Nicole asked as she stood in front of Mo Money, with her hands folded across her flat stomach.

"I'm good, the question is, is your girl okay?" She asked as her head came up. She still had her cute smirk, across her gorgeous looking face.

"She's cool." Nicole whispered as she stood there, really seeing what I saw in the young, beautiful female.

"Good, now what's next?" She asked.

"Nothing, you did good back there. What I need for you to do now is to just fall back, chill. Go on back to the hotel with the rest of the crew."

"But." She went to say, but Nicole placed her index finger on the young lady's lips, preventing her from speaking.

"No but's, just listen. I've already got you too far involved in what it is that we do," Nicole explained as she stood there.

"What do you mean?" Mo Money asked with wondering eyes.

"Nothing, Mo Money, I'll explain it to you later. Now is not the proper place nor time. Now hurry up before you get left behind."

"For real?"

"Yes, for real," Nicole muttered as she watched as Mo Money made her way through the club. Then saying to herself.

'Yeah, you're going to make a good Murder Queen one day, young lady. One day.'

Little did any of us know, that day was right around the corner…

Chapter 21
Forever!

At first Mo Money wanted to go with Nicole and the other ladies, but once Nicole had explained everything to her, she knew then that she meant business. So she hurried up and fixed herself up, then ran outside to catch up with the rest of the ladies, before she got left. She had just made it to the Denali as she climbed in between Strawberry and Entyce, when Mignon surprised her and turned her head and said,

"Hey you, my bad back there. You did a good job back there in getting the guys attention. I'm sorry for going off on you."

"No problem, I know how things can get when you're under a lot of stress and pressure," she politely said as she smiled back at Mignon, then began counting her money.

"That's what's up, just do as your told and you will go far in this group," Nicole remarked as she was climbing into the passenger seat of the truck, with the rest of the group.

Nonetheless, Mo Money was actually getting the feeling that she was being groomed for something more dangerous than being a world famous, Florida Hot Girl.

"Alright, which one of you ladies have dates lined up?" Mignon asked as she turned to look at the rest of the ladies inside the truck. "Everyone who already had a date, left already Mignon," Tameia spoke up from the rear of the truck as she sat in between Peekachu and Suga Bear.

"Okay, cool. You guys hold up for one moment while I take care of something real quick," Mignon said as she stepped out of the truck and walked up to the driver side of the truck Marquise felt so proud of.

"I wonder where her hot ass is going?" Suga Bear asked as she looked over at Peekachu.

"Looks like over to that blue bad ass truck right there," Peekachu answered, her eyes trying to see as well.

"Whoever the nigga is sure looks like money." Suga Bear quoted.

"I know that's right." Peekachu agreed. All the other girls knew what was what. A few minutes later, Mignon was back in the driver's seat.

"Okay ladies, I'm going to drop you guys off back at the hotel, while me and a few of the ladies have to meet some guys for breakfast." Mignon versed as she started up the truck.

"No problem, I can't wait to get back to the room so that I can get some sleep," Lil Redd said as she sat near the back of the truck, counting up her money…

In the meantime, Marquise didn't want his plan to fall short of completing, so he had told Mignon and her crew to meet them over at the Waffle House, right next to the Red Roof Inn Hotel, where the ladies were staying. And where he had kicked out almost close to fifteen hundred dollars for their stay for the entire weekend. It only took the girls approximately thirty five minutes to get back to that side of town and drop the girls off. Then they were parked right behind the blue Ford Expedition. "Alright ladies, leave your weapons inside the truck. Hopefully, nothing pops off inside the restaurant."

"You sure about this?" Nicole asked from the front seat.

"Positive. If anything happens and I pray it doesn't, we'll have to handle it outside. We don't need any innocent bystanders being hit by any stray bullets."

"I know that's right. And we especially don't want the same outcome here as we had in Daytona Beach," Strawberry remarked as she surveyed the area.

"You're right, Berry," Entyce stated.

"Now, can we all just get inside and enjoy something to eat with these clowns, since it's the last meal before their last meal, that they're going to have to pay for," Mignon said as Strawberry, Entyce, Nicole and Lil Tameia exited the truck, walking inside to Marquise and his party of goons; as if they were the baddest females on the planet. Truth be told, they were. The problem was that the guys who they were about to have breakfast with, didn't realize it at the time. Who knows, maybe they did know that they were in the presence of those females, known as The Murder Queens!

***

It was early Saturday morning as Rhynyia was the first one to roll out of bed. At first, she had forgot that she had come into my room in the middle of the night and fell fast asleep, so it took her a few minutes to realize where she was. "Your ass could have taken it easy on me last night, Michael," she said as she playfully punched me in my arm.

"Don't act like that my dear, you must have forgot that, it was you who wanted it."

"Whatever," she said to me, with me still laying there half asleep, dreaming of being back in Orlando, with my girls. "Wake your ass up, we have to get ready for the funeral." She then said to me, now waking me up completely. This is when I lazily turned over, slightly opening my eyes, staring at her as though I was still dreaming and if I was, she looked just as beautiful in my dreams, as she did in real life.

I was still half sleep and partly trying to get back to my dream, when Firstborn rumbled into my bedroom all un-announced and shit, with, "Yo baby boy, what time are we supposed to be leaving for the funeral?" He seen Rhynyia, butt ass naked. "Oh, excuse me, I didn't know that you were in here!" She looked at my shocked faced brother as he witnessed poetry in motion. I jumped up so quick out of bed, anger laced inside of my voice with,

"Hey, man, your ass don't know how to fucking knock!" I was livid as I abruptly jumped in front of her naked, luscious looking body, causing her to fall back onto the bed.

"No problem Firstborn, I was just leaving," she said as she smiled, then hiding a portion of her body under the satin sheets from my bed. Shen then reached for her silk night gown and placed it around her body, all the while as he stood there gazing at what any man would call the most gorgeous sight that they had ever seen. "Baby, be ready by eleven thirty please." She uttered, then kissed me softly on my right cheek and walked right past Firstborn, who was still somewhat mystified by what his eyes had just witnessed.

Just as she walked to the door, his wide mouth ass turned back towards me and said, "Damn lil bro, she's fine as a mutherfucker! My gotdamn dick is rock hard just by staring at her fine ass!"

"Yeah, you said that already. I thought I told your ass about eyeballing my lady, Firstborn?" My lips curled up as I stared at him, standing there, looking stupid.

"Mike, c'mon man. What was I supposed to do, the bitch was standing there without any damn clothes on?"

"First of all watch your foul ass mouth. She's not a bitch and there won't be too many more times that I allow you to call her one. Second of all, you should've took your bald headed ass back out of my room, until she got dressed, nigga!" I angrily said to him as I stepped out of bed, walking towards the bathroom, to take a morning piss.

"Whatever my nigga and miss all of that fine ass body of hers?"

I was still pissing, holding my manhood as I titled my head back, yelling through the door. "Hell, with the way I saw you putting her sister through all that pressure last night,

I can't tell." He started smiling, while showing off the few gold teeth inside of his mouth, saying.

"Man, she's alright and all, but she's not Rhynyia."

I had just turned on the shower, when I stuck my head from around the door, asking him, "Yeah, I hear you. So, what was it that you wanted?"

"Hey, listen. I forgot to pack some socks, please tell me that you have an extra pair that I can borrow."

I casually wrapped my towel around my body and walked back out into my room, then looking inside of my suitcase. "Here you go bro, you can have those socks," I said to him as I threw the socks at him. Due to the last time that he borrowed something of mine, without me knowing he had it, I ended up scratching for two whole days before I realized what he had put inside my shorts. Now that his black ass wanted to borrow some socks, I was like, "Hell, you can keep them damn socks right there, forever!"

Chapter 22

Fuckathon!

As his ass stumbled out of my room, he stopped at the door and turned to look back at me. "While your bullshitting, I'm actually thinking about taking her sister Natasha back home with us." I fleetly turned back towards him and quickly muttered, "Yeah, whatever. You know good and damn well that her father is not having that shit, my nigga!"

He just looked at me and shrugged his shoulders, then saying. "Man, whatever, Pierre and I are cool as fuck!" There it was, he had said it, but I didn't hear what he said and didn't pay too much attention to his body language. I just cut the nigga a crooked smile at his conniving ass.

"Nigga, close my door with your country ass!"

"Okay my brother, when this country ass nigga has his fine ass daughter draped all over my arm, don't trip!" My door slammed as I went back to doing me.

Now his black ass might not have been right about one thing, but his ass was damn sure right about him and Pierre being cool with one another. It seemed as though Pierre and him had agreed to work with one another in his ever-growing drug empire. With my ass not knowing a damn thing about the corrupt plan Pierre had put together with his sadistic minded ass. This is how it went, as told to me later, by Rhynyia. Pierre had agreed to give Firstborn thirty keys of the precious White girl, powder aka Cocaine, at the very low price of twenty-five bands a key. Off each key that he got on consignment, he would pocket around seven bands. After that he would start purchasing his merchandise from him at a much lower cost. The deal was that every time he re-upped, the price would go down. The luxurious twin engine plane that had been slated on flying us back home, had already been loaded up with the powdered substance two days prior to us leaving the island. If only I would have known what had taken place between the two of them, I might have had the opportunity of saving my brother's life … Now this is where my love for my only brother would be tarnished forever. The one guy who I always thought that I could count on showed me his true colors. Even up to this very day as I sit here in this prison cell surrounded by all types of men. Always remember this, "Those who you do the most for, in the end, will surely give you their ass to kiss!"

11:30 am… I was tying up my white Stacey Adams, then standing to check out my appearance in the full length mirror. First thing I noticed was that my tie wasn't straight, so I adjusted it, then placed my gold tie bar underneath my white silk shirt collar. The elegant looking three-piece Julio London suit that I had on was fitting me like a glove, while the waves in my hair were laying down like they had been trained to do. Minutes later, I was finishing up the final touch as I dabbed on some of my Burberry cologne, which had the entire hallway smelling like myself. I knew then that my look and everything else were on point as I walked out of my room, headed over to Firstborn's room, just to make sure that he was dressed and ready to go. But before I could get to his room, I was met at his door with,

"Well hello, Mister GQ," Maylia said to me as she caught me off guard, with her radiant smile and gorgeous looking outfit. I passively looked down at her and then asked her.

"Now why do you say that, beautiful?"

She gave me her warm smile and carefully replied. "Because Mister Michael, you look like you could be a fashion model, with the way you are wearing that suit."

"Well thank you my beautiful, young lady. You look nice as well," I replied as she stood there gazing at me with her mouth, now open. She stood there dressed in a nice black dress by Victoria Valenuza. Her lovely hair was dangling from her head, with a nice part right down the middle. At first glance you would have thought that she was a full-grown lady with the way she was dressed.

"Have you seen my sister yet?" She asked me while I was just about to walk into my brother's room. "No, I was about to as soon as I checked in on my brother." Her face still held a smile as she grabbed me by my arm and said.

"Well in that case, let's go check in on my sister together." I'm glad we did, because it seemed as though Firstborn and her sister Natasha were in his room going for round two of their private Fuckathon! ... Lil fast ass Maylia must have known that her poor sister Natasha was in the room having her back blew out. That's why her lil fast ass wanted me to walk with her instead of me checking on his ass. I guess she was watching out for her sister, that's why her lil grown ass was standing outside of his door, acting like she was lost and shit.

Moments later, the both of us were walking inside of Rhynyia's room with her looking like the Princess that everyone knew she was. Her dress was a nice, smooth, silk Italian made dress that came right above her knees. On her head, she had on a nice Brazilian made hat that covered up her eyes, from the view of others. It didn't matter though, because she had her signature pair of Gucci shades on, that kept the sun and others from seeing her splendid looking eyes.

"Wow, you look amazing," I spoke, breath taken away by her sheer beauty, style and grace.

"Whatever Michael, you look good as well." She spoke back.

"So, who designed that dress?"

"It's made by a brilliant fashion designer called Shakina Giovonni," she uttered.

"It fits you perfectly."

"It's just a bit snug right here," she said as she pointed to her nice, phat sexy ass.

"Girl stop." I spat, then looking at her heels that she had adorned over her pedicured feet. The heels were made by Viktor Salinski. She looked marvelous as she stood there, staring back at me.

"Rhynyia, you look just as beautiful as your handsome soon to be husband," Maylia said to her with excitement laced in her voice.

Rhynyia's face held a slight smirk as she replied. "Whatever, lil sis, is everyone else ready, yet?"

"Not quite yet, let me go find out, I'll be right back," Maylia spoke and darted out of the room. I guess she was going to warn my brother and her sister. Just as her lil short ass hit the door, she was gone. Rhynyia was still standing, looking into the mirror, when she looked over to me and uttered, "That suit really looks good on you, boo."

"Why thank you, Princess, and might I add, you look good enough to eat right about now."

"Thanks," she said as she slowly sat back down, then I guess the pain of burying her only brother, subsided and took over, which made her begin to cry. I casually walked over to be by her side as she laid her head on my shoulders. Tears cascading down her face.

"Rhynyia the more you cry is not going to bring him back; you have to be strong for him and yourself. And especially for your family."

She then leaned her head back and said, "Your right, Michael, he would not want me to be crying over him like this. He would always tell me that I was much stronger than him. And that I would one day have to be the glue that held this family together."

"Alright then, now dry your eyes and gather your composure so that you can face your family," I said to her as she put on more makeup, to cover up where her tears had stained her face. Just as she had finished, there was a soft knock at her door. She paused for a brief moment, then yelled.

"Come in!"

"Rhynyia, have you seen Natasha?" Her sister Countess asked as she walked into the room, looking like she was next in line to take over the family throne.

"No, did you check her room?"

"Yes, I've been there twice already."

"Oh, I'm sorry, hello Michael?"

"Hello, Countess," I said as she smiled back at me.

Then she said something that caught me and Rhynyia completely by surprise. "Boy, don't you look nice, in the same kind of suit that father is wearing today as well."

Rhynyia and I both looked at one another with wandering eyes.

"What?" Rhynyia asked with disbelief written all over her face.

"Father has on the same kind of suit. That is a Julio London suit, right?"

"Yes. and please tell me that your lying?" Rhynyia asked with authority in her voice.

"I'm serious, Rhynyia. I just passed him in the hallway looking for Natasha."

"Oh shit! He's looking for her ass too?" I asked in a panic.

"Yes," Countess answered as she went to walk out of the room.

"Shit!" I yelped as Rhynyia looked at me and asked.

"What, do you know where she is?"

"Follow me!" I reached out for her hand, then made my way down to my brother's room ...

Chapter 23
Shark Bait!

As soon as we got to the door of where my brother resided while there on the island where we both were visitors in her part of the world. Her sister Natasha was coming out of his room, while pulling her skirt down at the same time. Rhynyia was shocked just as much as I was as she observed her sister's lustful actions, then glaring over at Firstborn; before turning her cold stare in my direction. Without any hesitation, I shouted out,

"What? I'm not the one fucking her hot ass!" Rhynyia just continued her gaze at me and replied.

"I know, but he's your fucking brother! Do you know what would happen if my father found them out?"

"No!" I uttered, then came back at her with.

"She's your sister, so I guess the both of their retarded asses would have to explain their own silly actions to him." I voiced as everybody stood there waiting on someone to make sense out of everything.

"So that's what you're going to tell my father, Michael?"

"I guess and please remind me again, why would I have to tell him anything in the first damn place? And besides, I'm not the one who put their dick in her!" I was real cocky at that moment.

Rhynyia then stared back over at her sister, who was standing there with her index finger stuck in her mouth, laughing at the entire, awkward situation.

After a few seconds of us being frozen in time, Rhynyia gave her sister a very cold stare and uttered. "Father is looking all over the house for your ass go before he finds you up here like this!" Natasha looked at us and then back at Firstborn, before kissing him on his cheek.

"I love you, Firstborn," she stated as she pulled her lips away from his cheek.

"Oh my goodness, what did you do to her, Firstborn?" Rhynyia asked him, still shocked by what she had just heard her sister say to him.

He then nonchalantly turned around to face Rhynyia, forming his lips up he uttered. "The same damn thing that my brother did to your fine ass. I put this dick on her muthafucking ass!" Just as the sentence had rolled off of his very chapped lips, Pierre walked into the hallway. "Where is your sister, Nyia?"

"She was with me, father. I was helping her with her makeup."

Pierre then looked over at me and then back at Countess. "Nice suit you have on there, Mr. Michael."

Nervously I replied. "Yes sir, it seems that way doesn't it?" Even though his suit was slightly different than mine, it still had the same cut as the one I had on. I could tell by the way he walked with his back straight up only signified two things in his neck of the woods. The brother didn't play with his money nor his fucking family. And now that Firstborn was fucking with his daughter only meant one thing. He had crossed the line.

It was already bad enough that I was with Rhynyia and had her knocked up with child, but now this fool was fucking his second daughter and about to be playing around with his precious product. I had just turned around to look at Rhynyia who had already started walking back towards her room. As soon as the both of us were inside, she slammed her door shut, then turning to me with tears in her eyes.

"You and your foolish inconsiderate ass brother may want to leave as soon as the funeral is over." Confused and startled by what she had just said, caused my words to stumble out of my mouth as I asked her.

"Why, hell I didn't do anything?" Here I was thinking that she wanted to spend as much time with me as possible. But now that my brother had crossed that invisible line, our time in her part of the world was being cut short.

"I know, it's not you, Michael, it's your damn brother. I feel as if he stayed here any longer on the island, that his ass might do something so stupid that he ended up as being turned into shark bait!"

Damn, there it was. She had said it, but what me and her didn't know was what he had already signed up to do. Neither one of us knew that the poor dumb son of a bitch, had signed his soul over to the devil himself…

By now she was seated on her bed, wiping away her tears, when I placed my hand on her back. "Damn, so it's like that, huh?"

"It's not me Michael, it's just the simple fact that my father is very protective over his children. And your brother has definitely crossed that line."

That's when I sat next to her with my head held down. There was no way that I could allow her to crush my feelings like that, so I tried to act bold and said. "Your right, hell, I have a business to run and I damn sure can't run it while I'm over here."

"No you can't baby and I sure as hell don't want my father killing you and your crazy ass brother." Then, just as I was about to stand up and walk out of the room, there came a knock at the door. Then, a deep voice came behind the knock.

"Princess, you in there?" Her Uncle Lorenzo asked as he continued knocking at the door, before he slowly pushed the door open. He saw me standing there as he walked in, holding out his hand, so that we could embrace one another. "Hello, Michael."

"Hello, sir." I replied as I took his hand, then embracing him. The next thing I did was to walk past him, so I could go inform my brother of what had just took place inside of Rhynyia's room. "Excuse me, I'll let you two talk, while I go check in on my brother."

"Go ahead, Michael, I'll be with you in a second," she addressed me as I walked away. Just as I got to the door, I heard her uncle ask her.

"Are you okay?" I could hear him bluntly as I closed the door behind me. I paused for a brief moment, standing there listening to their conversation. While standing there I got that funny feeling that I had seen him somewhere before, but where? I asked myself as I stood outside of her room with doubt clouding my already confused and troubled mental state. It was minutes later, when it finally dawned on me as to where I had seen his distinctive looking face before. But was I certain that it was him that I saw that day. It had to be him and I had smelled that same fragrance that afternoon inside of the one particular clothing store. The same exact store, where I had those ten extra suits tailored to fit me. He was the man in the window, that same man that was looking down at Rhynyia and I the day we were out shopping for my suit. The question now was, was he there to purchase his suit as well? And if so, why didn't he make himself known while we were both there?

It wasn't until I walked away from her door, that I began to put the pieces to the puzzle together. By the time I reached my brother's room, I was sure of why his ass was there at the store that day. I just had to make sure that I had the right answer. I was still livid with my brother, so I didn't even bother to knock as I burst in, catching him standing there in his mirror, desperately trying to fix his tie. Something I would find out later, that he never wore.

"Listen Firstborn, you have to really chill the fuck out, my man before her father finds out about you and her sister."

"For what?" The bitch is fucking grown, isn't she?" He asked me angrily as he turned around, looking like our father in the face.

"Yes, she is grown, ole country ass nigga, but that ain't the fucking point!" I replied, while staring him directly back in his deep, cold, black eyes. "Man, that chick was a fucking virgin and I guess that she was supposed to only fuck the guy she was going to marry!" He turned away from me, seeing that I wasn't afraid of him anymore, the way it was when we were both kids.

"Man you sound fucking crazy. If the bitch wants some of this good ass country dick, well my nigga, I'm gonna be the be the nigga who she gets it from!

Chapter 24
Shirt Collar!

I had to calm myself down before the both of us started fighting with one another over something that I really couldn't control. That's when I took a few deep breaths, then looking at him. "You just don't get it, do you?"

"Get what, hell nah! I guess I don't get what it is I'm supposed to be getting, my nigga. I guess that every pretty bitch that come around, Michael Valentino, is the only one who's supposed to fuck her, right?" He stood there with a side smirk on his face, waiting for me to answer.

"Nah, that isn't it James." I was so mad that he had me calling him by his government name. "Whatever Mike, that's exactly what the fuck it is, so stop fucking pretending that it isn't. Man, I'm not stupid by a long shot. Ever since I have been here with you, your always fucking the bad ones, when I get the left over bitches. Well not anymore, lil brother. I want to fuck the top notch bitches too, my nigga!" I was stuck for just that brief moment as I actually seen a few tears well up in the bottom of this nigga's eyes, before saying to him.

"So that's how you feel, huh?"

"Yep, that's exactly how I fucking feel, pimp!"

Now this is when I had the look in my eye when in the movie Purple Rain, Billy, the club manager, told Prince about his music and Prince jumped up from the chair inside his dressing room. I even had my index finger pointing at him when I angrily replied. "Now, how many times have I told your black ass about the pimp shit?"

"Whatever, my nigga, it is what it is," he said. That's when I went for the door, stopping at the entrance and turning around to say. "Man, you're fucking crazy, just hurry up and get ready! We're already running late and don't let me hear you call me a pimp again!" I walked out of his room, filled with anger and hate, without even hearing what he had to say. Even in the end, when those fake ass agents came to interview me, some twelve years later, they asked me the question if I was a pimp. And to this very day, I would always tell anyone, that no I wasn't a fucking pimp. But the fucking government labeled me as one. So to all that read this book, you will see for yourself, not one damn time in any of these books, will you ever hear me reference myself as one...

Just as I stepped out of my brother's room, Pierre was standing there looking like my fucking twin brother, simply because of the same suits we were wearing.

"Ahhh Michael, there you are. I'm glad that you're okay, I couldn't help but overhear you and your brother arguing from inside of his room."

"Nah, we weren't arguing, we were just discussing a few things of importance, that's all," I replied as I tried to erase my frown with a fake smile.

"Good, because if we are going to be business partners, we do not need you two brothers to be fighting amongst one another," he said as he walked up closer to me, smiling.

"Wait a minute, what business partners, Pierre? I don't remember agreeing with you about any business deals."

At that moment, he had me fucked all the way up.

He looked at me, with those cold eyes of his and uttered. "Well, that is not what your brother said to me, when he agreed to move thirty keys of my most precious product, back to Orlando." He was now rubbing his hands together, as if he was expecting me to give him some of my money right, then and there.

"Fuck!" I shouted in pure disgust. Not only had this rock headed nigga been fucking the man's daughter, but he had agreed to sell his cocaine as well. "I know Mr. Michael and if his black ass defaults on my money or my precious product, you will be witnessing another funeral at you and your families expense." The man spoke with pure confidence.

"Hey, wait one fucking minute. My family has nothing to do with what you and him agreed upon," I spoke. "I never agreed to deliver your product, so you can count my black ass out of whatever type of deal you and him agreed to!" I was still yelling as I stood my ground.

Rhynyia must have heard the anger in my voice as she dashed out of her room, with her Uncle Lorenzo closely behind her. "Michael, Father, what's going on out here?" She yelled as she looked from me to her father.

"Tell her Pierre, go ahead and break her heart with the news of how you and my crazy ass brother have made a deal about your cocaine. And make sure you include the fact that I have nothing to do with it!"

She couldn't believe what she had just heard as she lunged for the neck of her father. Grabbing him right up under his chin, then yelling. "No father, you promised me that you wouldn't involve Michael in any of your drug trade deals!" By now, she was sobbing and crying hysterically as she held onto his shirt collar…

Her father very forcefully grabbed her by her arm, causing her to succumb to his strength. Once he witnessed her slight fall to her knees, he stood firm and uttered.

"I know what it is I said, but I never said anything about his thirsty, naive ass brother. Now stop your damn crying and get ready to bury your damn brother!" The man was cold hearted and evil, not to mention that he just didn't give a fuck about who he hurt or crushed along the way. I guess a way that all cold-hearted business men were. I stood there, frozen stiff as I watched this man, who on the day that he was to bury his only son and all he cared about was his precious white powder, that my idiotic brother had agreed to sell for his ass. At first I thought about lunging for the man myself, but with his two big henchmen standing off to his side, that dumb ass thought quickly vanished completely from my confused mental state of mind.

Him and his brother Lorenzo lazily turned and walked away, never turning back to see how Rhynyia was doing. When they all had stepped a few feet away, is when I bent over and helped her up from off of the floor. She dully stood to her feet, heartbroken.

"Now I remember why my dear mother left my father and me with him. He was very abusive to her and she wanted no part of the line of work that he was into." I finally had got her inside of my room and gently laid her onto my bed. It was then when I heard some arguing outside of my window. So I lazily walked to my window, to see her Uncle Lorenzo, talking loudly with Senior Chulo'. At first, it took me a moment to hear what they were saying to one another, so I slightly opened the window as I faintly heard him say to the old, fragile man.

"As long as my secret is safe, we should both be okay."

"Be easy, my good man. No one seems to know what happened to Prince Naheed," Senior Chulo' replied as he looked up into the dismal looking cloudy skies.

"And no one ever will." Lorenzo recited as an evil grin emerged upon his cold-hearted face. The man was just as dirty as his brother Pierre was. So nasty and foul, that led me to believe that he and his brothers were up to more than just selling cocaine. Right then and there, I knew that there was no way that I could allow Rhynyia to bore me a son, my first son and have him living there with her evil-minded family…

***

Now you could just imagine how I felt, while riding to the funeral with her family, now that her father had made a threat against my very own family. He might not have realized it, but I took it as he was talking about my immediate family, who had no idea of what my brother and I were up against now. All I could think about were my mother and father, not to mention my sister and my two daughters. Did he know of them, and did he have his people already back in Florida, watching them? I didn't know how I could tell them to be very suspicious of any funny looking people who they didn't recognize. But for now, I was going to make sure I watched every move Pierre made, while I was still over in Puerto Rico.

The funeral procession slowed down to almost a halt as all the cars and fancy SUVs pulled in the distance of the large cathedral. Since I had proposed to Rhynyia, I was allowed to ride in the first car with the family, while my knuckle headed brother rode behind with the henchmen. The place was crowded with her family and the locals from the surrounding area. If you didn't know who was being buried, you would have thought that it was some big-time celebrity or something. Or even the president for all that mattered with the way the cathedral and parking lot were packed with people. Just as the stretch limo came to a halt, we were told to stay seated until the bodyguards surrounded the limo. My head was on a swivel as I began to look around for any would-be attackers. Rhynyia was up under me as if I was the one who needed protection. That's when I casually leaned over and asked her,

"Damn, it's that serious huh?"

"Yes Michael, even though were at my brother's funeral, there just might be someone here trying to become famous by taking one of my family members out."

"Damn!"

"Yes, damn is correct young man. So, are you sure coming into my family is what your heart desires?" Pierre asked me as he sat still, smiling and staring at me hugged up with his daughter.

"I wouldn't have it any other way, sir," I replied as I held my ground.

This is when she leaned closer into my body, softly whispering. "Thank you. And no matter what happens next, please remember that I will always love you," she spoke as if this was going to be our last time together. Now she had me fearing for both of our lives, right there at that moment…

Chapter 25
Walnut Stained!

The funeral didn't last that long, only about thirty minutes, which surprised me. I mean just as the Priest did his thing and said a few words, we were all rising to our feet, which caused me to lean into Rhynyia's ear with, "So it's over already?"

"Yes, Michael, unlike your customs and beliefs, we are a much different people."

"I see. Wow, that was quick."

The next thing I knew, we were all outside at the gravesite. So as I stood there silently with her and her family, watching the attendants lower her slain brother down to his final resting place. She dully reached out for my hand, but with me seeing that her knees were about to buckle; all due to her becoming weak from witnessing the casket being lowered into the cold, deep black hole.

I reacted quickly by placing my stern arm around her instead, preventing her from falling face first into the hole with her dearly departed brother. After she gained her placidity, she leaned into my ear,

"Thank you once again, my legs seem to have given out on me. And I didn't want to make a spectacle out of myself by falling down into that hole. They all would have probably thought that I was trying to join my brother."

"No matter what, always remember that I will always be here for you, no matter what," I recited while looking over across at my brother, who was hugged up with her sister as though he really cared about her and her grieving family. Truth be told, he cared for no one but himself.

As I stood there, watching him through my dark Gucci shades, I had never realized that he held so much resentment and animosity towards me. If it hadn't been for the argument, I still wouldn't have known the full amount of hatred he kept bottled up inside of him. Don't get me wrong I had always knew as young kids, how he always tried to garner more attention from our father, due to him feeling like I was much closer to our father than he was. All because our father married my mother instead of his mother. His anger only grew deeper as time went on, due to him not having a father figure around to watch him grow up into a man. Now, he saw that I had grew up to become more like our father, than he did, he felt as though our father groomed me, instead of him. How wrong he was, our father loved the both of us. Sometimes I felt as if he loved him more than me. I never expressed that to him, due to me knowing that he would just say to me. Whatever and then blow me off. So I kept that feeling to myself. None of it mattered now, we were both there with Rhynyia and her family, watching them lower their loved one six feet deep into a black covered hole, then filled with dirt, which had to be the hardest thing to do as I stood there observing their father, Pierre Santiago.

Especially since he was a man with so much pride and ego, that had to bear the ungodly sight of burying his only son, who was supposed to one day take over the family business. In which Rhynyia, the very next in line would have to do if anything happened to her father.

Something that she had made very clear to her father, that she wanted no part of. The reason she danced was only to make her own money, so that she didn't have to depend on her family's dirty money. She had vowed on that somewhat cold and misty day in November, that she would never devote her life to being part of the Santiago drug smuggling cartel. So as the walnut stained casket met its final destination at the bottom of that hole, her lovely stepmother and the rest of her sisters, threw in a rose and watched them sluggishly fall onto the walnut stained casket, trimmed in gold...

The Priest had just said the last goodbye, as the family and I walked away, I guess them realizing that they would never see Prince Naheed again. As far as I was concerned, I hadn't ever met the brother before, so how could I miss him. All I missed at that moment was getting back to Orlando, so that I could be amongst my family, the world-famous Florida Hot Girls.

Firstborn walked ahead of me, still tightly holding onto a crying Natasha as I walked alongside Rhynyia, who seemed to be holding up okay. Up ahead were all the stretch limos and black Range Rover parked right behind one another, waiting for the family to enter into them once again. And then bear the painful ride back to the estate. This is where the immediate family would gather to eat and reminisce about their loved one. On the way to the particular limo that we rode in, I happened to ponder the peculiar relationship between her Uncle Lorenzo and Senior' Chulo. I wanted to say something to Rhynyia, but thought it was best not to, since she was looking a bit weak, from that day's events.

But as we got closer to our limo, out of my right peripheral vision I caught the glimpse of something shining through the trees. My first instinct was that it was a hit, so I quickly whispered into Rhynyia's ear.

"Bae, I think it's a hit!"

"Where?" She asked as her head went on a swivel.

"Right over there, in between the trees!" I spoke back to her.

The next thing we knew, she must have had a gun tucked inside her dress, because she quickly shouted out. "It's a hit, get down!"

Everyone fell, while Pierre grabbed his wife and youngest daughter and leaped inside the limo. Leaving Rhynyia and Natasha standing there.

Tat-tat-tat-tat-tat! Both of them began firing rapidly at whoever was inside the tree line. Me and my brother ran for cover, right behind the limo. Good thing the limo was bulletproof, because what happened next still remains a mystery to me. The one big bodyguard that walked with us that day shopping, hit the car with his right hand.

"Get Pierre and his wife out of here, now!" He shouted, leaving me and my brother in the open.

"So, you still want to be in this family now, nigga?" He asked me, spittle flying from his mouth.

"Hell yeah, why wouldn't I? Now give me a piece, so I can fire back at who's shooting at us!"

"Sorry playa, I only brought one!" He yelled back as he ran up beside Natasha and began blasting. People were running and trampling over one another, with my black ass out in the open, without a fucking piece. Rhynyia seen me after she had fired off a few rounds and shouted.

"Natasha, hit whatever or whomever is in the tree lines! I have to protect Michael; he has no weapon!" She shouted as she darted back, where I stood, or should I say crouched down.

While that was taking place, her and Firstborn sent a barrage of bullets at the culprits. Just as Rhynyia got over to me, she stared me in the eyes.

"You good?"

"Indeed, now get me the fuck out of here!"

"Follow behind me!" She instructed as we made it over to one of the Range Rovers. In the driver's seat was a dead driver, right next to him was Senior' Chulo.

"How in the fuck?" I yelled as Rhynyia pulled the driver from the Rover and slung him to the ground.

"Get your ass inside, fuck him, he's already gone!" She shouted as I did as I was told.

Just as I got in I opened the glove box, hoping to find myself a weapon.

"What the fuck are you doing, Michael?" She asked me as she started the Rover, then put the Rover in reverse.

"Trying to find me a fucking gun, that's what!" I shouted back.

"Well there's no need to look in there, why would his old ass have a gun in the first place?" She asked as she then slammed the Rover in drive and got the hell out of the cemetery. Leaving Natasha, Firstborn and the rest of everybody else back there.

"You know, you do have a point there," I remarked as I watched how she was wheeling the Rover in and out of traffic.

"I know I do, now buckle up, we don't know if we're being followed or not!"

That was the first thing I did when I got inside the truck. Put on a damn seat belt. She must didn't know that her crazy ass half-sister Sharon, had me in a predicament just like this one, a while back.

"So, were you hit? She asked, frantically driving in and out of the heavy traffic.

"I don't think so!" I replied as I checked over my body. Then looking back at her. "No, I'm not hit. Now who do you think it is that was shooting at your family?"

"Probably the same people who are responsible for the death of my brother."

"Damn, so they shoot at your family at his fucking funeral?" I asked, with concern laced in my voice.

"Death doesn't have a specific place or time when it comes for you. You just have to make sure that your right with the heavenly father, when it reaches your front door step," she stated. Damn, Rhynyia really had a way with words.

"What was that?" She asked me as if she had read my inner thoughts. "Nothing, just that you have a way with words."

"I know. Now let's hope and pray that I can get you and your brother back home safely. We wouldn't want the both of you to be killed over here on the island," she said as she continued driving, headed back to the estate.

"So, what about my brother and your sister? You think they're going to be okay back there?" I asked, praying that they would be.

"Trust me, he's in good hands if Natasha has anything to say about it."

Just as she said that, she pulled out her phone and dialed a number.

When the person on the other line picked up, she shouted through her phone with, "Maria, did everyone make it back to the estate okay?"

"Yes Rhynyia, they're all here. Where are you and your sister, Natasha?"

"I'm inside Senior' Chulo's vehicle. Natasha and Michael's brother are back at the graveyard."

"Your father wants you all back here right now! Whoever killed Naheed, is trying to take out the entire family."

"We're on the way. Were there any casualties?"

There was a brief moment of silence, then Maria came back with. "Your Uncle Lorenzo has been shot."

"Oh my God, how bad is he?"

"We don't know right now, all we can do is pray for him, Princess." A single tear dropped out of her eye at that very moment. "Fuck!" She yelled as she slammed her fist down on the steering wheel.

"Princess, are you okay?" Maria asked.

"I'm Gucci. Me and Michael will be there in the next ten minutes!"

"Okay, Princess, drive safely." Was all she said as she hung up.

At that moment, I was glad that I hadn't said anything about my immediate speculations, between her Uncle Lorenzo and Senior' Chulo. I didn't want to be wrong about what I was thinking about the man, neither did I want to cause any commotion between her family and I. So I held my intermediate thoughts to myself. Besides, I had other things on my mind at the time. First it was the shocking news of me finding out about my third daughter, Mykel, then it was the awful secret of me knowing exactly who Rhynyia's mother was. Not to mention who her sister was. Last but not least, was the constant reminder of Sharon being at home alone, carrying my child.

I took a deep sigh, then let it all out, while still gazing out of the window, thinking to myself that my brother and I hadn't spoken to one another since the argument back at the house.

"Oh well!" I mumbled to myself as she continued speeding, trying to make it back to the estate. My complicated mind continued to slowly drift back and forth between the girls back home, my brother's safety and our presence with the Santiago family.

"Are you okay, Michael?"

"Yes Rhynyia, just going over some things inside of my head.

"Okay, I only asked because I thought that I heard you say something. Don't worry, your brother is safe with Natasha. Besides, he looked like he was pretty well taught with firearms," she said as she cut me a half smirk. "Yeah, that he is, Rhynyia. That he is...."

Chapter 26

Jacksonville, Florida
5:15 am
Early Saturday morning …

After the ladies had ate breakfast with Marquise and his goons, they went back to their hotel room, in which he had paid for and went to sleep. Marquise tried every trick in the book to convince Mignon and her crew to let them upstairs for some sexual activities. But Mignon, knowing of their deadly plan to kill them, promised him that it would be better for them to all get together after the club, later on that night. All he could do was to agree with her wishes, so after two hours of him pleading and begging with her to change her mind, with no avail she stuck to her guns, as it took her forever to give him a kiss on his fat, nasty looking cheek.

Just as the ladies walked into the hotel lobby, she stopped the few ladies with her. "Hey, let me have those room keys real quick."

"Why, what's wrong now, Mignon?" Entyce asked, eyes wandering from Mignon to the rest of the crew of deadly vixens.

"Just trust me on this one. If those guys paid for our rooms, then they can always come back here and say that they lost their room key, then when the manager or front desk clerk gives them another key, they can come into our rooms while we're asleep and do what they want to us," she said, to a wide eye group of ladies.

164

"She does have a point there, ladies," Tameia spoke as the women did as they were told...

Meanwhile, while driving away from the hotel, Marquise looked over to Punkin, who was riding shotgun inside of the blue Ford Expedition.

"Man, when I get my hand on that ass later on tonight, I'm gonna fuck the dog shit out of her fine red ass! Then I'm gonna sit back and enjoy every minute, while I slowly kill her and the rest of them hoes!" Marquise shouted as he beat his steering wheel with his open palm.

"What about waiting for the nigga in charge of them bitches?" Punkin asked as he passed the blunt that he was choking on. Due to every time he took a deep breath, the herbal substance caused his small, frail body to jerk as if he was having a seizure or something.

"Fuck that! I'll just have to cross that bridge when I come to it."

"True, say less then," Punkin remarked while having a shitty ass grin on his face.

"Now why in the hell are you shaking like that, my nigga? Is there something wrong with my weed or something?"

"Nah cousin, you know my ass has bad asthma and shit. I really shouldn't be smoking this shit."

"Well stop."

"I can't," he said as a half-smile appeared on his face in anticipation of receiving the blunt again. "That's crazy."

"What?" Punkin asked.

"If something was killing my ass every time I smoked it, I think that I would have enough sense to stop."

"Whatever nigga, anyway. What, you my damn daddy now?"

"Who knows, you just might be, my son," Marquise versed as he laughed.

"Whatever. Anyway, that Mignon bitch was fine as hell, wasn't she?" Punkin asked as he grabbed at his crotch area.

"Hell yeah, all I could do when we were eating breakfast was just stare at her lil sexy ass, while trying to control my dick from jumping out of my damn pants." A red eyed Marquise said as he tried to navigate his truck through the early morning traffic.

"But what about the one they call Mo Money? Now that lil thang is fine as hell!" Punkin recited as he turned slightly to retrieve the blunt back from Marquise, who seemed to be coughing just like his lil homie.

"Yeah, she was alright and shit, but not as fine as Mignon. I wonder why her lil fine ass didn't come eat with us?" Marquise replied as he slid the blunt over to his partner.

"I have no idea there partner. But let me ask you this though? Did you see the lil female that Rasheed fell for?"

"Did I? I was eyeballing the bitch the entire time that we were eating. I think that's the one who I'm gonna kill first, for trapping my dude with them sexy ass eyes of hers," Marquise uttered as he looked over at Punkin real hard. "I hear you, all I know is that we should run trains on all of them fine ass bitches, you know, like tie their asses up and just fuck'em all week long!"

"Damn, lil ass nigga, you just want to be fucking on some killer ass hoes all week and then kill their ass?"

"Yep," Punkin said as his face held an evil grin. "You know what would be downright shitty though?"

"Nah, what?" Punkin asked.

"If somehow we could find somebody that has Aids and then have that nigga fuck all of them bitches, raw!" Marquise said as his mind started searching for that someone. "Damn my nigga, you one cold hearted nigga!"

"Damn skippy, my nigga. You know what we should really do?"

"What's that?"

"Go back to that hotel and tell the front desk clerk that we lost our hotel keys. She or he couldn't do nothing but give us another key to each room that I already paid for. Man, we could rob them hoes and kill their ass at the same damn time," Marquise stated as he sat at the traffic light, right down from Black Magic on Beaver Street.

"Nigga you done lost your rabbit ass mind! Them hoes gone know it was nobody but our ass. And besides, the rooms are in your name, so when them hoes come up dead or missing, your black ass is the first person there going to want to speak too, silly ass nigga!" Punkin remarked.

"Yeah, you're probably right. And those hoes are smart enough, that they probably already changed out the room keys, to every one of those rooms. We might as well wait until tonight after the club," Marquise stated with a sour taste in his wide ass mouth…

Chapter 27
Around Ten!

The two close friends had just stopped at the last red light before Black Magic, when Punkin looked over at his boy and asked. "So, what's up? You know someone for the shitty job of giving them hoes Aids, after we fuck them?"

"Nah, not right off hand, but whatever the case might be, we're still going to meet them hoes tonight after they leave the club."

"How?" Punkin asked, heart beating fast. He never really had to kill anyone, so now with what his friend wanted to do to the girls, was very luring to him as he sat in the passenger seat, eyes wide open.

"We're gonna lure their ass to the old warehouse where my brother had them two other hoes at and then go from there," he spat with vengeance in his malice heart. Punkin began to smile as he looked over at Marquise.

"Gotcha bro, hey, drop me off at my car. I know my lil bitch is going to be mad at me for coming home so fucking late. But we had business to tend to."

"Your right. I'll meet up with you and the fellas around eleven o'clock tonight, so that we can go ahead and take these hoes out of their misery," Marquise recited as he slid over in the right lane, so that he could make a right turn off of Beaver Street. This is where Punkin had left his lime green box Chevy. It was ducked off behind the club. His small beady eyes lit up like a Christmas tree just as Marquise pulled into the parking lot. All due to a few crackheads, who were admiring his car and twenty six inch rims. "So, what's up, them basers with you my nigga?"

"Hell nah. Hey, y'all fucking basers get from round my goddamn whip, before I start busting caps off around this bitch!" He shouted as he leaped out of the truck, waving his pistol in the air.

"Tell 'em again, partner!" Marquise shouted as he laughed at the way the last baser fell to the ground, then jumped up, all while trying his best to pull his pants up. Punkin then turned back to his homie. "Man, that last baser had some hops, didn't he?"

"Yes his dirty ass did. I think that was the nigga Larry Hester from Middleton who used to run track. That nigga still fast as hell, ain't he?" Marquise asked as he stood outside of his truck, still laughing.

"Yes he is, with that long rectangular shaped ass head," Punkin replied.

"Hey, I'm going to get a haircut around ten and then back at the crib to get some sleep. So I'll see you at eleven tonight, right here at the club!"

"One." Marquise shouted as he jumped back into his truck, headed to his house, still thinking of his grimy ass plan.

***

Meanwhile, the Murder Queens had already put their plan in action. The time was around nine twenty in the morning, when Mignon and Nicole pulled back into the parking lot with a nice ass rental truck. "Alright, go inside and get the others, so we can get to the spot to snatch up that lil ass nigga," Mignon recited to Nicole, who was posted up inside the Denali.

"Hold on, I'll just make a call," she said,
"Go ahead."

Minutes later, Strawberry, Entyce, Nicole and Tameia were all walking out of the hotel, dressed in jeans with black hoodies over their heads. "Morning ladies," Mignon voiced as they all stepped inside.

"Hell yeah, what's good?" Tameia asked.

"Nothing, it's just time to make the doughnuts!"

"You got that right, girl," Nicole smirked as she slapped Tameia on the hand. Mignon then sped out of the parking lot, headed to their intended destination. Thirty minutes later, they were parked off to the side of a closed down establishment, lurking, trying to stay out of sight. Mignon then turned to the backseat.

"So Entyce, are you certain that this is the barbershop where that lil nigga be getting his hair cut at?" Entyce then turned her head to the right, then the left, before she uttered.

"Yep, I'm sure it's the right one. Just hold your horse, I'm pretty sure that his ass will be here. What time do y'all have?"

"Nine forty five."

"Thanks Nicole, me too. His girl claims that he gets his haircut here every Saturday morning, around ten. Right fucking here!" Entyce voiced.

The ladies had been sitting, waiting on their lonely prey for about five long minutes. Eating and chilling, when Mignon turned to the backseat and said,

"Okay ladies, listen up one more time. Nicole, you're going to lure his lil short funky ass over to the truck, once he gets his head to the passenger window, Strawberry, you pull that four nickel out on his unsuspecting ass. And then were going to put his bitch made ass inside of the truck without anyone noticing a damn thing! Then, we're going to take his ass to that old warehouse where they took Chyna and White Chocolate. Tameia, you follow behind us in his car. Then, we're going to take his short ass inside and torture him before his boys know what hit their ass, understood?"

"Yeah, we got it, Mignon." Strawberry voiced as their victim turned the block, right on time.

"See, ten AM. Just like she said!" Entyce voiced from the backseat, wiping crumbs of her Sausage McGriddle away from her lips. A startled and somewhat shocked Strawberry had just realized that something awful had happened, when she shouted.

"Hey, where in the hell is my gotdamn hash brown?" The entire truck became awfully quiet as all eyes turned to stare at her.

"For real, Berry?" Nicole asked, trying to refrain from laughing at her crazy ass.

"Yes, my ass is hungry as fuck!" The girls all burst into laughter as Entyce shoved her hash brown into her side. "Here bitch! Eat this!"

"Thanks!" Strawberry uttered as she began stuffing her mouth with her food.

The ladies then turned their attention to watch as Punkin stepped out of his freshly painted, lime green Chevy, with what he had on from the previous night, stumbling and tripping as he tried to walk to the front of the barbershop.

"Alright Nicole, you're up. Do your thang," Mignon stated as Nicole jumped from the truck, looking just as good as she did the night before. She was any man's dream. But right about now, she was Punkin's worst nightmare.

"Hey Punkin!" She yelled from across the street. His head slightly turned to the left, then to the right as he tried searching from where the voice came from. Then, his eyes got a glimpse of the female he had only saw a few hours earlier. Only this time, she was calling out his name, loudly. This is when he placed his hand over his eyes, preventing the sun from witnessing sheer beauty at its best. At first he had to squint his eyes, making sure that his eyes weren't playing tricks on him, while looking across the street, smiling.

"That can't be her?" He said to himself as he saw her standing there, looking like a nice piece of ass.

"Well it looks like ole boy is about to be fucking early this morning." He thought with his dick and sprinted across the street, almost getting hit by a few cars as he made his attempt to get next to her. Not realizing that this was the same mistake that Rasheed had made.

"Over here," she said as she frantically waved him over. His swag gave his sexual intentions away as he got closer, then saying.

"What's good, lil mama?" His face still held a smile as his eyes undressed her. "You, I was hoping that we could get together before you got your haircut."

"Damn, lil mama. How you know that I be getting my hair cut here around this time?" He asked as he began to survey his surroundings, now thinking that his lady had tried to set him up.

"Don't worry about that, boo. Let's just say that I've been watching your fine ass for a while now."

His mind started thinking as he quickly came back with. "But I thought that we were all getting together tonight, after the club?"

"Yeah, we are, but I'm trying to see what you're working with before the rest of the girls find out."

Once again he started smiling, not realizing that Strawberry was slowly placing her chrome four nickel up against his small ass temple, while wiping her mouth as well.

"Hell, I'm down. What's good then? You want to hop in the ride and we go back to the hotel?" His face still holding onto that shy smile he had. The same one that Lil Kitty had fell for.

"This four nickel my nigga! That's what's good, bitch made nigga! Now get yo fuck ass inside the truck before I smoke that ass right here in the middle of these streets!" Strawberry yelled as though it seemed like she was still a bit hostile by the way he had treated her a few weeks prior…

Chapter 28
Corn Beef Hash!

Poor Punkin, his two eyes were as big as Grandma's country flapjacks when he seen the barrel of the four nickel, up against his small ass temple.

"Damn lil mama, y'all ain't got to treat a pimp like this and shit!" He voiced while shaking and slowly entering the truck.

"Whatever nigga, show me a real pimp," Nicole said as she turned her nose up at the man.

"Right here lil mama, you're looking at one," he recited as he thought that it was a game.

"Nah, what we have here is a dead man, walking," Mignon recited as she placed the truck in drive and pulled off. Right then Punkin realized that it wasn't a game as his small head was turning from side to side, while staring at the cold unit on the faces of Entyce and Tameia. "Okay, now that we have him inside, grab his keys out of his hand, Tameia." Mignon barked as she slowly drove over to where Punkin had parked. Just as they got to the side of the establishment, Tameia jumped out of the truck with keys in hand. She then quickly hit a button on the key chain, to hear the chirp sound, letting her know that the doors of the car were unlocked. "You good?" Mignon asked as her short ass adjusted her small frame behind the steering wheel.

"Yeah, right behind you guys!" She shouted as she looked around inside of the nice interior the car had, then turning the key in the ignition to hear the roar of the 350 engine.

"Damn, this bitch nice. I might have to cop this bitch!" She said out loud as she turned up the sounds, blasting Hit 'Em Up by the late great Tupac. She then placed the car in reverse, once she had backed the car up, she slammed the bitch into drive, following right behind the girls. All while bumping her small head to the beat of the four 12's he had pounding in the truck of the Chevy. Sounding like a got damn college band. FAMU to be exact.

"I know one thing, she better not fuck up my car. I just had that bitch repainted," Punkin shouted from the backseat with his hands tied up.

"Nigga, that's the last thing that you need to be worried about, because after today, there's a good chance that you won't even see that piece of shit car, ever again!" Strawberry recited, while looking at Punkin seated between her and Entyce.

"Shit, he won't be seeing that car again nor anyone else for all that matters! We gone put an end to all this shit, tonight. You better believe it!" Nicole said as she slowly turned her head back to the front.

"Fuck!" He shouted out in disgust. Mignon then drove down Washington Street headed straight for the warehouse, with Tameia closely following behind her, driving the shit out of Punkin's freshly painted, nice looking whip. All the while poor Punkin was squirming and frantically trying to get out of his situation. When Entyce noticed all the movement he was doing.

"Oh, so your ass just can't sit there and be the fuck still, can you?"

"Man, fuck you! You think I'm about to just sit here and be the fuck still, while you hoes think about how y'all gonna kill my black ass?" He angrily asked, sweat pouring from his brow.

"No problem bitch ass nigga, I know what to do!" Entyce shouted as she placed a cloth filled with ammonia over his small ass mouth. Seconds later, his small head fell back as if she had just punched his ass.

Twenty minutes later, they were all pulling up to the warehouse with a butt naked ass Punkin and his nice lime green Chevy.

"Come on Nicole, let's see how to get inside this bitch!" Mignon voiced as her and Nicole got out, leaving Strawberry and Entyce behind to pull his ass out of the backseat. But right when ole Berry began to pull at his half naked ass, she made a gruesome discovery.

"Hey, I hope that you hoes know that his lil short funky ass must have been so fucking scared that he did something foul and awful, all over himself?"

"What makes you say that, Strawberry?" Mignon asked as she yelled back to Strawberry as her and Nicole were still trying to look for the entrance to get inside the warehouse.

"Because the lil nigga shitted all in his fucking boxers and over the seat, where his ass was sitting!"

"That's what I was smelling, I thought that was your ass back there farting and shit!"

"Fuck you, Nicole!" Strawberry replied, angrily. While Nicole was laughing so hard that she tripped over some rotted out wood, while Mignon shouted back.

"Well I be damned. Take his shirt and start cleaning that shit up!" Strawberry and Entyce were still trying to get him out of the truck, while looking at each other with a look on their faces as to say to one another. "Hell you looking at me, for, I ain't cleaning up that nasty shit! Looks like his ass ate some corn last night!" Entyce uttered.

"His ass did, hoe. Remember at breakfast this morning, his ass had some corn beef hash! Strawberry voiced as she began searching for his shirt. "Bitch, there is no corn in corn beef hash!" Entyce shouted as she started laughing at ole Berry. "So why in the hell do they call it corn beef hash, then? If there is no corn in it?" Strawberry asked as she let his head fall to the hard ground.

"How in the hell am I supposed to know? Bitch, just pick the lil nigga's head up and come one. One of us is going to have to clean that shit up!"

"Won't be my red ass!" Strawberry replied as she picked his head up off of the ground.

Moments later, Mignon and Nicole had just found the entrance to the gutted out warehouse. The place reeked of stale air and death inside as the both of them used all their might and slid the door back. The two ladies stood there with their hands covering their mouth, when Mignon looked over at her partner. "Looks like someone or somebody was planning on doing some foul shit up in here, later today!"

"Yep, it's kind of creepy in here, isn't it?" She asked as Entyce and Strawberry slid Punkin's shitty ass in between the both of them. All while Tameia stayed at the entrance of the warehouse, making sure no one slipped up on them.

"Ewww, what did his ass eat?" Nicole asked, while coughing from the foul stench. "Strawberry said that the lil nigga had corn beef hash at breakfast."

"Thanks Entyce, I was only kidding," Nicole uttered while trying to fan away the foul smell.

"Yo, tie his lil shitty booty ass up over there and make sure that his ass can't get away!" Mignon voiced. Just after they tied him up, the ladies did a quick walk through the warehouse to make sure that they could use the place for what they had in store for the rest of the dirty gang.

"So, what do you think?" Mignon asked.

"The way I see it, it's all we have and besides, since them niggas brought our girls here, it fit's to bring the head nigga and his goons here," Nicole sputtered.

"She's right Mignon," Entyce voiced.

"Sounds good, hey, where in the hell is Strawberry?" Mignon asked as they all started looking around. "Over here guys, just making some last minute changes to our boy's unfortunate situation. You know, showing the lil nigga how it feels to have something engulfed inside his ass. Maybe he won't be defecating around here anymore today." She said as she walked over in their direction, smiling an evil smile.

"C'mon, ole Berry, what did you do to ole boy?" Nicole asked as her face held a smile.

"Nothing, let's just say that his ass won't be releasing his bowels no time soon. Now let's ride, did you hoes forget that we have a meeting to be at?" Strawberry asked as they all looked at their expensive timepieces on their wrist.

"She's right, let's ride," Mignon uttered while they all rushed for the door. Just as they got outside to see the sun trying to reach its peak. They all looked amongst each other. Then a hot and sweaty Tameia yelled out. "So, what about the niggas car?"

"Yeah Mignon, we just can't leave it here. Someone might ride by and get suspicious," Entyce voiced.

"Yeah, okay. Tameia follow us back to the spot. We'll just have to have it there with us. If someone sees it, they will just think that he's there with us," Nicole voiced.

"Good, because there was no way in hell that I was going to ride in that backseat with that shit all over it," Strawberry yelled as she jumped in the front seat of the Chevy. "When you get back, make sure you park it across from the hotel. We don't need security cameras from the hotel seeing one of us pulling up in the car."

"Good idea, Mignon."

"I know, now let's get out of here."

All the way back, Nicole kept complaining about the smell that Punkin had left behind. "Entyce, I thought that you guys cleaned out the truck?" Nicole asked Entyce as she looked back at her with her two fingers pinching her nose closed.

"We did. That lil nigga must of had more than just some breakfast food. Smells like he had some barbecue too!" Entyce remarked while laughing.

"Whatever, Entyce."

"That's what your ass gets for always wanting to ride in the front seat." Nicole turned and gave her dear pal a nasty ass look, while Mignon continued driving back to the hotel, before the rest of the team woke up or even arrived back from their individual dates ...

Chapter 29

Small, Beady Ass Eyes!

The meeting amongst the ladies would only last for about an hour, before they would strike out for the Arlington Mall. This is what they did before every show we had, while out on the busy highways and byways. You know, just a bit of shopping before they went to perform at the various clubs. Punkin on the other hand would be held at the warehouse all day, sleeping, not even realizing would spectacular events that were being held in their honor, later on that night. The only people that would actually miss the young man would be his crackhead customers that he would serve to throughout the day.

Punkin was just the first of Marquise goons that would feel the pain and abuse that the Murder Queens were about to inflict on their individual bodies. So while Marquise slept through the day, he didn't know that the rest of his crew would be picked off, one by one. Then taken to the same warehouse he had in store for the ladies. All his big ass knew was that his goons were all out or home, getting ready for the night's events.

Flash, the next goon in charge was at home, sleeping too. Dreaming about fucking Entyce later that night, before he put a Taurus 9mm bullet in the back of her head. If only he knew that was in store for him that day. Maybe, just maybe he might not have bothered on waking up that somewhat cool, misty day in Jacksonville, Florida.

Then there was his partner Carlos, the third goon in charge, who was just happy to be included in the mix. With a resume that only held the fact that he was just another low life type goon, the type of goon that would do just about anything to make a name for himself. Once he witnessed how fine and attractive the ladies were, all he wanted was some free ass. And he felt that if he helped with the demise of the ladies, that would not only get a name for himself, but a free shot at a nice piece of ass as well. If only he knew what Marquise was getting them all into, he might have thought different about the entire situation. But it was way too late for all of that, the Murder Queens were all in now. So you see, there was no turning back, once they had put together their elaborate scheme, that would help them get away with all of their deaths and wouldn't have to worry about Marquise ever haunting them again. Or at least that's what they thought, but as we all know, everyone doesn't always get away with murder, or do they? That's a question that still remains a murder mystery.

***

Short ass Punkin woke up sometime around one thirty that afternoon. At first, he thought he was in a bad dream or something. It wasn't until he opened up his weary tired, dried eyes and began trying to untie his hands. It was then that he realized the awful truth, his black ass wasn't in a fucking dream, but something far more serious than that. This is when he looked down to see that his hands and arms were tied behind his back and that his size five feet were bound as well. They told me that they had hogtied the short man. He knew then that he was in a very bad position, once his eyes witnessed his unfortunate predicament that he was in. Every time he tried to wiggle himself free, he felt a sharp agonizing pain coming from somewhere in the lower portion of his small brittle body. As he continued to try and break free, he asked himself.

"Where in the hell is this damn pain coming from?" At first, he thought that maybe he had been shot or even cut deep somewhere on his body. But after looking down that thought was quickly banished from out of his perplexed mind. So with twenty minutes of him laying there, all tied up, he realized where he was. The warehouse. Now only if he could remember how he had got there. A few moments later, he knew how all of what he was going through, transpired. "Those fucking bitches. They're the ones who brought me here!" He said to himself as he laid there with hot tears escaping from his small, beady ass eyes...

As he laid there butt bunky ass naked, without any of his fucking clothes nowhere to be found. He pondered what those sick ass females had in store for his ass. This caused his mind to plague him with all kinds of scenarios. But what had him curious, was the constant pain of a foreign object, plugged somewhere inside of his small body frame. He simply just laid there with all kinds of mad thoughts running back and forth. Then he thought of how the same females had cut off the penis of Marquise's baby brother and shoved it into the mouth of Rasheed's cousin. The pain, hideous thought of that alone, caused him to quiver, then shake violently as he laid there. He then slowly looked down to make sure that his manhood was still attached.

"Oh thank God!" He said to himself. He would have said it out loud, but his mouth was taped shut. It didn't matter though, he was just elated to witness his three inch manhood still intact, all shriveled up, staring back at him.

While still trying to make the correct observation over his rickety body, he just couldn't get a feel for where the punishing pain was coming from. That wasn't until he tried to relieve himself of some very irritating gas. At first he thought that he was just tripping, until the gas wouldn't pass through his now swollen rectum hole. "Oh shit! What have these bitches done to my black ass?" He muttered as he started to cry all over again. His small eyes then began to swell as crocodile tears escaped from the well of his eyes and rolling down his cheeks, with him thinking of where the pain was actually coming from.

Unbeknownst to him, the ladies had stolen the one thing that he had never imagined being taken away from him. You see, placed deep up inside of what used to be his small asshole, was a size twelve inch dildo inside it. It had become the most extrasensory pain that no man in his right mind would want to bare. Then to make sure that he didn't or couldn't push the dildo out of its new home, Strawberry had covered his asshole tightly with some black duct tape. After he realized what the ladies had did to him and his asshole, he fainted. It wasn't until he heard the sound of his phone ringing in front of him, that woke him up. His phone had been placed right in front of him, so that he could see who was calling. When he woke up from hearing the phone, he passed out again, when he witnessed the picture of the person calling him. Due to it being a picture of his girlfriend Tracey and their precious little three-year-old son, Martevious Quinshon Williams Jr. aka Lil Punkin Jr.

If only he would have listened to Tracey when she told him about being so predictable, he wouldn't be laying there on that cold, cement slab, butt ass naked with twelve inches of a rubber dick stuck so far up his ass that every time he moved, he felt awful, agonizing pain. Something that his partner Flash was about to feel as well...

* * *

Now the ladies were at the Flea Market first, shopping and some getting their hair done, when your girl Strawberry spotted Flash walking through the side entrance; with two of his homies from the club. She quickly snapped her phone from her waist and hit Mignon on the hip, by paging her on her Nextel phone. "Yo, where you at?" She asked as she came straight through her phone.

"What's up, Berry, what you got?"

"Yo boy just walked in."

"Who?"

"Flash and two of his homies."

"Cool, stay on his sweet ass and let me know when they separate."

"True," Strawberry said as she placed her phone back onto her waist, then walked behind the three guys, keeping a close eye on her mark…

Chapter 30
His Name!

The plan was simple, they were going to grab Flash and then take his ass to the warehouse, before even being missed by the rest of the Hot Girls. Which was a very good plan as the Flea Market began to overflow with the Saturday crowd of people, out shopping for the night festivities. That's what we all loved about Jacksonville. No matter what, there was always something to get into.

Thirty minutes into Berry following Flash, he happened to break off from the company of his two homies for a brief moment, when he saw one of his local homosexual partners, by the name of Hush Puppy. This was who Flash slept with from time to time for some extra cash.

Hush Puppy was given that nickname all because he kept his gay interactions completely on the down low. Like R. Kelly said, "Keep it on down low, nobody has to know." So in other words, no one knew his business but him, the father upstairs and the men he chose to sleep with. Flash tried to convince himself that he only went out like this when he needed some extra spending money, but truth be told, the homie was living the life of a bisexual male. "Damn, Flash!"

By the time that the Murder Queens had snatched his lil thin ass up, the other girls were off busy doing their thing inside the Flea Market. The Queens threw Flash in the back of the Denali, with him thinking that it was a game as well as Punkin did. He was actually laughing out loud, when

Strawberry pulled down his tight ass dickie shorts. "What are you hoes doing?" He asked as he smiled at Strawberry.

"You're about to find out lil homie, just chill," she uttered as she pulled out another size twelve dildo. Strawberry was a real bonafide freak. His eyes grew larger with the anticipation of the dildo entering its new place of residency. But suddenly his smile disappeared when him and the ladies saw the large various shit stains that were smeared inside of his dingy, white boxers.

When he witnessed the nasty ass unit on the face of Strawberry he quickly uttered out loudly as he held up his lone index finger.

"Wait a minute, before you insert that inside of me! These boxers belong to my little brother, you see my mother hadn't had a chance to wash clothes yet."

"Nigga please, you know damn well that these are your shitty ass boxers that you have on. You're the only child nigga!" Strawberry said to him as she slapped the shit out of him with the butt of her chrome four nickel. As his head fell back, she abruptly took out her tape and then wrapped it around his large ass mouth. Then she shoved the dildo up his already large rectum. Little did they know, Flash had a smile as long as a banana on his face, underneath the duct tape; while he lay there welcoming the entrance of his new found friend.

"Damn, if I didn't know any better, I would swear this lil thin ass nigga's ass has already been tampered with, especially with the way this dildo slid so easily up in his large ass hole!"

"What I want to know is, what is up with you shoving dildos up these nigga's ass?" Mignon asked as she pulled out of the parking lot, headed for the warehouse.

"Hey, if you would have been there the night these nigga's tortured my ass, you would know why. Now drive this muthafucka like your black ass just stole it!"

"Yeah, right bitch," Mignon said as she turned back to the front, smiling. "I know one thing y'all hoes better make sure that this nigga don't shit all over Mike's fucking truck."

"Whatever Nicole, if he does, your cleaning this one up, since you're fucking the cool ass brother."

"Whatever, Strawberry," Nicole answered as a genuine smile came across her lovely face at the mere mention of my name…

***

Meanwhile, Mo Money and the rest of the ladies were busy spending their bread that they made the night before. Smiling and laughing amongst one another as they all walked throughout the busy Flea Market, not just turning heads, but breaking muthafucking necks. Chazz and Richard were standing on the outside, smoking and choking on some Purple Kush weed, while Suga Bear and Peekachu were on the inside, trying to find the right outfit for the club.

JK and her crew were busy telling the guys what club they would be dancing in for the night. While your girl Lil Kitty was still trying to get in touch with Punkin.

"Damn, I wonder why his lil stupid ass isn't answering his phone?"

"Who, Lil Kitty?"

"The lil short ass nigga named Punkin. He's the one who paid for our rooms this weekend and we're supposed to be hooking up but Ms. Mignon told me to fall back."

"Why?"

"Hell, I don't know, Chyna. Something about she didn't feel right about the lil ass nigga."

"Umph, you know I did see her and the rest of them chicks that she always be with talking with him and the gang of niggas he be with."

"For real?" Lil Kitty asked, causing her to now question Mignon's moves and instructions. "Yep, by the way, have you seen any of them in the Flea Market?" Lil Kitty looked around with her nose up in the air.

"You know, come to think about it, I haven't," Lil Kitty voiced as her eyes stopped wondering.

"I really think that them hoes are up to something no good, if you ask me," Chyna stated.

"Me too Chyna, me too."

Now while those two deliberated on what some of the girls were up to, Tiger and her cousin Monique were over at the nail salon getting their toes and nails done, while the beautiful Charlie B and her waitress friend were busy trying on a new pair of stilettos. Your girl Heidi was off somewhere buying her lil hard head son Denzel, some shirts for the upcoming school year. While Tarshay, the one who thought that she was smarter than everyone else in the group, was busy off inside the Flea Market bathroom, taking care of one of her many customers who just couldn't wait until later that night to see why she was always in high demand. Tarshay was a mean piece of work...

***

Over in Puerto Rico, off of that small island, tucked away from others, Firstborn and Natasha had made it back to the estate, unscathed. After all the commotion ceased the family went about their business as planned. The immediate family ate and talked about Prince Naheed, while Firstborn and I were busy packing our bags. After all what had took place, we both decided to leave that evening. Mainly because Firstborn could get Pierre's cocaine back to Florida unnoticed. Rhynyia and her sister were going to fly back with us, but would be staying on the plane. They had to get back to help assist in finding the people responsible for their brother's untimely demise. Even though Rhynyia was showing, she still insisted on being there for him and her family.

I didn't have a problem with her helping them, due to me knowing how much her brother meant to her, besides who was I to stop her from finding the people who had robbed them of his presence. All I wanted to do now, was to get back to what was at stake. Which was my lucrative business of having one of the most sought after groups of strippers in the world. The world famous Florida Hot Girls.

My brother on the other hand assumed that the faster his ass got back to Madison, Florida, the quicker he could get his drug business off the ground. He would enlist the help of a few friends and then hit the streets running. The time was around six thirty and all of the guests, family and friends had left the compound, when Rhynyia came to me with,

"Hey you, are you and your brother ready?" her voice sounded a bit raspy as I slowly turned to her and said,

"Yes, I guess so," I recited with a part of me not really wanting to leave her side as of yet. But the other part of me wanted to leave just as soon as I had got there.

I then put the rest of my things inside my bag and walked down stairs with Rhynyia, holding tightly to my hand. We had just got midway of the lengthy stair when I heard my brother and her sister following behind us. I was still too upset with him to turn around and say something, so I pretended that I didn't hear him and continued walking. Don't get me wrong, I was glad and thankful that he and her made it back to the compound safe and not hurt. But a big part of me was still haunted by what he had agreed to do with Pierre.

Rhynyia and I had just got to the bottom of the staircase when I could hear Pierre and his brother Felix in the living room, talking. He stopped all suddenly when he saw us, then turned to us, yelling all out loud and shit. "Rhynyia, the plane is all fueled up and ready for departure, how long do you think all of this will take?" He asked while walking towards us, with his face holding an evil looking grin...

Chapter 31
My Chest!

She then dully turned her head to one side, trying not to make eye contact with the man, she called father and said, "Once we drop them off back in Orlando, we shall be returning home, if we have no hiccups," she voiced, her weary heart troubled.

"Excellent my dear, Rhynyia." He then turned to me, eyes piercing through my inner soul. This right now would have been a perfect time for my conscience to show his face. But come to think about it all, he never showed up whenever I was with Rhynyia. But just as I thought about him, I remembered what he had told me when he first arrived on the scene. "I'm only with you, when she's not around to make the smart decisions for me." I was so deep in thought at the time that I didn't even hear what her father was saying to me, until Firstborn looked at me with tears in his eyes.

"Mike-Mike! The man is talking to you." My head and eyes quickly focused on him as he looked at me.

"Excuse me, what was that sir?"

"So I see that you and your brother are finally leaving us, Mr. Michael." His face still held that shitty ass grin that he always had. I then looked him squarely in his eyes as I stated,

"Yes sir, Mr. Santiago. I have to get back to my business. You do understand, correct?" I recited, while extending my hand out to him, so that we could shake hands before we left the island. Then, without my paying close attention, he pulled me closer into him and placed his arms around my neck. Then he placed his mouth up against my right ear, before lightly whispering to me,

"Please don't fuck up my money or my precious product, Mr. Valentino. For I would hate to have to send THEM over to Orlando to find you and your thirsty ass brother!" He was so fucking close to me that I could smell the cognac on his breath. This is when he let my neck go, while slowly walking away backwards, still having that grin over his face. I was rubbing my aching neck, then looking at him, asking him,

"Them!" I said it loud enough for everyone there to hear me. "Yes, that's what I call THEM!" He then rudely ignored me as he went to shake Firstborn's hand, then saying to him, "I look forward to seeing you again real soon, Mr. James Lorenzo Vallentino Jr." For some odd reason this is why I believe his ass was crying. He had heard the man say something about them. In between his cries, Firstborn gave the man a half a smile, I guess letting him know that he would be back with his money as soon as he had sold his product.

But as we were all still standing there, I wanted to know who in the hell were the people he called THEM. I assumed that he meant his group of hired Henchmen, not realizing once that he was actually talking about the ones who were standing only feet away. As we said our last goodbye to the rest of the family, it was off to the private air strip that he owned some ten miles away from the compound.

It was already around seven thirty, so we would get back into Orlando around nine that evening or at least that's where I thought we were headed to. So as we pulled away from the villa in one of the customized Range Rovers, I thought to myself that if we made good time, I would still be able to make it to the club in Jacksonville, if I played my cards right. Perfect, I could get back and then get to my precious team of elegant, exotic, beautiful females, who I missed more than the air I was breathing. But what kept beating me across my head was what Pierre said about them. Who were they and were they already located in Orlando? So as I sat there, head down, mental throbbing, it had me in a really bad place.

Like I said, the air strip was only ten miles away, so we arrived there in no time. The door to the luxury private jet plane was already open, so we all stepped from the car as a few of their men came and placed our luggage on the plane for us. We all got on board and to our seats as Miguel had the engines already on, waiting for us to board the plane. Minutes later, we took off from the vast island, me and Rhynyia hadn't even said a word to one another all this time as the plane ascended higher into the partly dark night. But over to themselves, Firstborn and her sister seemed as though they couldn't get enough of each other as they kissed and cuddled just as soon as the doors of the plane closed. Just as the fasten your seat belt sign went off is when I laid my head back, trying to get me some needed rest. I must have dozed off ten minutes later, while my Queen had fell asleep as soon as her head laid up against my chest...

***

As Sharon sat alone in her front living room, watching television and casually glancing over at her young daughter, Bre, she couldn't help but think about Michael and wonder when would he back home with her. She hadn't talked to him since the other night and still didn't know if he was returning that day, or Sunday.

As she sat there, she tried her best to keep a free mind, but for some odd reason, she felt as if someone or something was lurking for her, right around the corner...

***

A few miles across town, her mother was still dealing with her secret past that her and Pierre only knew about. She was now left with the daunting task of actually telling Sharon about her past or just take her secret to her grave. The only thing wrong with that someone other than her would have to die not knowing about her other daughter. Her mother now sat alone in her bedroom, staring at her phone, pondering on what she should do. Then without thinking about it another moment, she picked up her phone and dialed her daughter's number. The phone rang once and she thought about just hanging up, before Sharon answered it. But she couldn't do that. If she did, Sharon would just hit "Star 69" and call her back and besides, Sharon had caller ID.

So the phone rung two times before Sharon decided to pick up.

"Hello, mother." Sharon answered, sounding in a pleasant, tranquil mode. This startled her mother for a brief moment.

"Hey Sharon, you busy?" Her mother asked, tears beginning to form in the well of her eyes.

"No ma'am, just sitting here waiting on Michael to call me. I guess whenever his ass decides to come back home," She replied as she crossed her legs, while she sat on her leather black sectional.

Her mother took a deep breath, then gathered her emotions as she let out a deep sigh of relief. "Listen baby, there's something that I need to tell you."

"Okay mom, I'm all ears," Sharon said with a smile. Her mother then began to tell her about her life as a young lady, while living in Orlando and club-hopping with her childhood girlfriends.

"Ma, now why are you telling me about when you were young and out at the different night clubs here in Orlando?"

"Because Sharon, I don't know how to tell you this," she said as she paused, then Sharon cut back in with,

"Tell me what ma?" The moment and the air just stopped all of a sudden, when she asked again. This time with urgency in her voice. "Ma, tell me what?" She asked, in what seemed like a light panic.

"Sharon, I had another child before I had you."

This is when Sharon eased up in her chair, then placed her hand over her mouth, before she asked out loud. "What?"

"I had another child before you," her mother spoke. "I heard that part, so what did you have, a girl or a boy? Do I have a sister or a brother?" She asked as she stood to her feet, with her stomach feeling like it was still seated inside the chair.

"You have a sister Sharon, and I really don't know where she lives." Her mother then paused again as her tears cascaded down her lovely face.

"So, you're telling me that I have an older sister and you never felt like you should've told me about her?"

"Yes, baby."

"So, why are you telling me this now, after all this time?" Sharon asked as she stood there, hands on her hips. Thinking that she heard something outside of her front door.

"Yes, but that's not all," her mother said.

"What, there's more?"

"Yes, I think that I might even know who she's seeing."

"Who's she seeing? What does who she's seeing have to do with me?" Sharon asked as she walked towards her front window, curious about the noise she heard only minutes ago.

"Mom, say something!" Sharon screamed into the phone, due to her mom being quiet.

Then, just as if lightning had struck, her phone went dead. Sharon went into a panic as she quickly tried to call her mother back. While she frantically tried to dial the number, there came a knock at the door. Sharon sensed that something was wrong, so without cautiously thinking right, she opened the door without asking who it was. But when that door opened up, standing on the other side of the door was none other than the badly burned face of … the next sound that Breanna heard was … "Booooom!"

Chapter 32
Handle That!

Back over in Jacksonville, Florida … The ladies were all dressed and ready to leave for the club. The time was somewhere around nine forty five and they wanted to get there so that they had enough time to dress in, so when the first dollar dropped, they would be there to pick it up. Mignon and Richard both pulled up in the parking lot around ten twenty, with Mignon dropping off all of the ladies, but keeping the Murder Queens with her. Just as all of the ladies stepped out with their bags in hand, Mignon looked over to Nicole, then placing her hand on her thigh. "Hey, Nicole, I need to speak with you real quick."

Nicole looked at her friend with a warm smile. "Yeah, what's good chick?"

"Keep an eye on the girls until we come back."

"So you want me to stay here?" She asked as she sensed the urgency in her friend's voice. "Yeah, you know, in case we don't make it back. Then you can be the one to tell him what happened," Mignon said with a bit of doubt on her mind.

Nicole gazed into her friends eyes, both women knowing that this could all go wrong if not handled correctly. "Please don't think like that, chick. When has there ever been a problem with any of our deadly missions?" Nicole asked, the entire truck went eerie silent as Strawberry, Tameia and

Entyce sat there, motionless. They were actually having a bit of doubt themselves, but their faces didn't show it.

"Yeah, you're right. But you know, there's always a first time," Mignon said as it looked as if she wasn't sure about something. It's like a dark cloud was hanging over her head at that very moment.

"Well, don't let this be that first time for failure, my friend," Nicole said to her friend, then looking over at the rest of the crew.

"Indeed," was all that Mignon said as Nicole asked her,

"So, how long before you all get back?" Nicole asked as she lazily eased out of the truck, then waited for Entyce to make her way to the front seat.

"Give us about forty minutes, give or take. If we're not back by then, something has definitely went wrong. And we're going to need all the help we can get," Mignon recited as she winked her left eye at her girl, then pulling away, looking back at the as the tires made a loud *skrrrr* noise when Mignon gave the high powered SUV some gas as she sped away from the club located on Beaver Street.

Nicole then somberly put her head down as she made her way past a few ladies who had just stepped out of a taxi cab, trying to beat the house curfew time. So they wouldn't have to pay an extra thirty dollars for being late.

"Hey, were you riding in that truck with them crazy ass hoes?" A slim bumpy faced female asked as she walked up behind Nicole with attitude.

Nicole dimly turned around, she was still feeling a slight pain inside her chest, from where she had shot herself. She quickly put on a half smirk as she looked at the female up and down. She then cocked her neck to the side. "What was that hoe?"

The bumpy faced chick, now felt some fire coming from Nicole, but she didn't want it to seem like she was scared.

"I said, was you riding with them crazy ass hoes who almost ran me and my girls over as we stepped out of that damn taxi cab?"

Big Keith, the guy that Milik had working on the door saw the fire inside the eyes of Nicole and quickly interjected with. "Whoa-whoa, hold on Nu-Nu, you don't want to take it there with that one, or either the other one who just walked in with her."

Nicole quickly turned around to see who Keith was talking about. When she did turn around, it was no one but the lil bad ass Mo Money.

"You good sis?" She asked, while smacking her gum, loudly. A sincere smile crossed Nicole's beautiful face.

"I am now, thanks for having my back, sis!" The both of them then glared over at Big Keith, then saying in unison. "Yeah, handle that, before we have to!"

Chyna was just lacing up her new three hundred dollar pair of boots, standing by the doorway of the dressing room, when Lil Kitty stopped and asked her. "Hey, did you hear what happened to those guys that took you and White Chocolate out and didn't pay y'all your money?"

"Yep, I heard some of these Jacksonville bitches talking about it as soon as we walked in," Chyna replied as she stood up, then placing her hands on her thick, soft yellow ass hips. "That's what them niggas get for fucking with me and my girl. Now let me ask your lil slim ass this. Did you hear about that nigga who got whacked last week in Daytona? How about his ass was from Duval, too?"

"Damn, for real?" Lil Kitty asked as she stood there with that same tired ass smile on her small ass face.

"Yep. Right muthafuckin' here from Jacksonville," Chyna remarked.

"You know what, Chyna? I might not be the brightest female in this group of ours, but I truly believe that some of these females in this group are actually the females who are going around killing people."

"Talking about them bitches called the Murder Queens?" Chyna asked, a serious unit on her light skinned face.

"Yes, girl," Lil Kitty spoke, face still with a fucking smile.

"Why you say that?"

"Think about it. Every time there seems to be a problem with any of the girls in this group, it gets dealt with, immediately and with life threatening consequences," Lil Kitty voiced.

Chyna then pointed her index finger at Lil Kitty, while saying. "You know your black ass just said a mouthful."

"For real girl, just think about it." Neither one of them didn't even see someone walking up on them, but they did hear her say.

"Excuse me, Lil Kitty, think about what?" Nicole said to Lil Kitty as she was trying to get through the dressing room door of the club. Nicole had surprised Lil Kitty as she stood there and paused for a brief moment. Trying to show Nicole that she wasn't intimidated by her sudden appearance. First she looked Nicole squarely in the face, swallowed deeply, then said, "I was just telling Chyna here that I believe that some of the girls in this group may actually be those females who call themselves the Murder Queens."

"Nah, Lil Kitty, that's not true boo. Those chicks, whoever they might be, are not a part of this group. I can assure your lil ass that. We're just a large group of ladies that shake their ass for a lil cash. So please get that notion out of your lil small ass head."

Lil Kitty wasn't the one to back down, so she countered with, "Okay Nicole, well where in the hell did Mignon and some of the other girls speed off to, just now?"

Nicole looked around the club as if she was looking for answers, when Mo Money stepped in with, "They had to go pick up a new chick that I met at the Flea Market, earlier today. The bitch claims that she wants to dance with us."

Nicole looked back at her girl, who was actually lying through her teeth. "Yep, that's exactly what they had to go do," Nicole said to a nosy ass Lil Kitty and Chyna as they all walked away, not believing a word Mo Money had just said.

***

Fifteen minutes later, Mignon, Strawberry, Entyce and Tameia were pulling up at the warehouse. They had changed trucks and were now jumping out of the Expedition dressed in all black. "Okay, ladies, let's make this real quick. We don't have that much time," Mignon stated as she looked around at the ladies. They had just slid the door back, standing there looking at the two tied up hostages, who were butt ass naked with duct tape wrapped around their mouth and ass.

Entyce ploddingly walked over to a butt naked Flash and kicked him directly in the head, then reciting out loud, "Wake the fuck up, nigga!" She then kicked him again, this time he woke up screaming or at least trying to scream, but his mouth was wrapped so tight that he could barely breathe. Flash then looked down to see that he was butt bunky ass naked with his manhood dangling from his mid-section area. Moments later, he received the shock of his young life, when he looked over and seen his small frail bodied partner, Punkin over in the corner with his ass taped up as well.

This is when he tried to get loose, but came to realize that his asshole was wrapped up tightly also. That's when the brother started moving around on the floor as if his ass was a giant worm. The motions that he was now making, had him feeling some type of pleasurable sensation of having something that size, engulfed up inside of his very large rectum. The girls didn't realize it at the time that all of this was taking place, but this is what Flash did. Inflict pain, inside one's ass. Mignon, being amused by his actions then walked over to where Punkin lay and ripped the tape off of his mouth. Just as soon as the tape was removed, he began spitting up saliva as she slowly ripped the tape from across his thin ass lips, making sure that she inflicted as much pain as possible to the young man.

"What in the hell do you think you hoes think y'all bout to do to us?" He screamed as he finally had a chance to talk.

"Showing your fuck ass just how it feels to be fucked in the ass, my nigga!" Strawberry yelled as she stood over his limp body. "Man, fuck y'all silly ass hoes! When my boy Marquise finds out what y'all bitches got going on, y'all hoes are gonna beg for us to kill y'all! Now take this very large play dick out of my ass!" He yelled, with spittle spraying from his angry mouth. The ladies might have wanted to listen to the young brother, because they were at the same warehouse where Marquise had planned on taking them too. Neither one of them knew this. Something that they might have wished that they knew, before it was all too late for them…

Chapter 33
Murder Queens Trouble!

Mignon stood there over her young victim with a malicious looking smirk on her face, just about getting ready to say something, when Strawberry took center stage and said. "What the hell ever and hell nah! Her, neither I is going to take that play dick, that stuck so far up your funky ass, that you can taste, out of your ass." She then got on her knees, placing her head up against his ears and said. "Now you see how that shit feels to have something shoved up your ass, don't cha? Shit doesn't feel so damn good, does it?" She then stood up, wiping her mouth of her built up frustration. Still watching Punkin as he laid there grimacing in sheer pain, head moving back and forth as he began to weep again; just like a grown ass baby. "Punk ass jit!" Strawberry voiced as she turned back, then placing her hands on her hips, still trying to think of what other method she could use on her young victim.

Meanwhile, inside a dark corner himself, your boy Flash on the other hand was actually enjoying every minute of the nice twelve in dildo, being submerged up inside of his ass. As he lay there, deep in thought, his mind drifting thinking that the dildo in his ass was his homie, Philly, up inside of him and fell back to sleep, dreaming of their many sexual interactions that they would have after drinking a few cold beers together. You see, every other Saturday after Philly got off work and had received his fat paycheck, him and Flash would meet over at the park and toss a few cold ones back. Just after they had finished the twelve pack, Philly would entice the young man to go behind their special oak tree that was located inside the park. Once there, Philly would have his way with his man. Then right after, he would hand Flash over about fifty dollars. Fifty dollars! Yep, that's right, fifty measly dollars. This is what it took for Philly to engulf the man's rectum.

Back over where Punkin lay, Mignon had just told Entyce, "Put some more tape over his mouth and we'll be back here with the rest of his crew after we leave the club."

"Cool," Entyce replied as her head went up and down.

"We good here, ladies?" Tameia asked as she had checked out the perimeter, then walking back inside to link up with them …

Twenty minutes prior, Marquise had been trying to get in touch with his boy Punkin for half the day. But when he got no answer, he knew that something had to be up. Now this man wasn't a dummy by a long shot. With that said, he kind of figured that maybe, ole Punkin might have tried to get some pussy without him, so he headed to the ladies' hotel. This was where he spotted his man's car, parked right across the street from the hotel.

But once he seen that there was no SUV there, he knew that something was off. He had just got to the club, when he happened to notice that half of the girls were there, but not the ones who him and the crew had breakfast with. This is when his curiosity got the best of his black ass…

Back over at the warehouse, once Tameia had asked the ladies were they good, Mignon assured them that all was good. Then saying to them, "Okay, we're done here, let's ride." But just as they got to the door and slid it back, smiling at one another. The scene played out in slow motion as they looked up, only to be looking directly into the barrel of their adversaries loaded gun.

"Fuck!" They all screamed in unison.

"I thought you checked our surroundings?" Mignon screamed at a scared shitless, Tameia. "I did!" She shouted back with fright and fear in her cute eyes. But it was the big guy, who confirmed what she did.

"She did bitch, but we were too clever for that ass. Now fuck, is what me and my partners are about to do with you and these hoes!" Marquise recited as he pushed the Murder Queens back into the warehouse. Punkin's little beady ass eyes lit up, when he seen and heard his man's loud ass voice. He had been rescued at least that's what his ass wanted to believe at that juncture of his young life …

***

Now remember how I told you earlier, that my conscience only showed up when I was without Rhynyia? Well how about, the only other time he showed up was whenever my ladies were in trouble …

"Mike, Mike! Man wake your ass the fuck up! Your girls are in deep shit!" At first I thought that I was dreaming. That was, until I woke up and witnessed my conscience sitting across from me, sweating as if he had been outside, running all damn day. I quickly wiped my dreary, tired eyes.

"Trouble?"

"What?" He asked as he slid closer off his seat.

"You said trouble, what are you talking about?"

"Nigga, your fucking girls are in trouble and by the way it looks, they won't be making it out of this one!" He stated as his head dropped.

I just sat there, shaking my head from side to side. "I knew something like this was bound to happen." I mumbled to myself, then easing my baby's head off my chest, while desperately searching for my phone so I could call Nicole. Just when I found it, I stood up, just about to call Nicole when Rhynyia must have sensed that I had moved.

"Michael, what is it? Is everything okay?" She asked as she yawned and stretched.

"Yeah, just calling to check in on the girls," I replied as I waited for Nicole's phone to ring. She answered on the first ring.

"Hello, Mike."

"Hey Nicole, what's good?" What she said next, only confirmed what my conscience was trying to tell me.

"I don't know Mike, but I think that the girls are in some type of trouble."

I sighed, then asked her. "What kind of trouble, Nicole?"

"Murder Queens trouble," she voiced with some urgency in her voice.

"Where are you?"

"Still in Jacksonville. The girls went to that warehouse where those guys took Chyna and White Chocolate that night. And they're not answering their phones."

I could hear the sadness in her voice. "Okay, calm down," I said as Rhynyia showed a look of sheer concern all over her face.

"I can't Michael. Mignon told me right before they left, that if they weren't back in forty minutes, that they would be in some type of trouble!"

"Damn!" I shouted, causing Firstborn and Natasha to wake up. "Mike!" …

Chapter 34
Flight 1256

There I was again, stuck, not hearing Nicole calling out my name in the background of my phone. I didn't snap out of my daze until I heard Rhynyia yelling through the plane. "Maria, change of plan! Have Miguel take us to Jacksonville! Pronto!"

"Yes, Senorita!" Maria replied as she ran towards the cockpit, full speed. I was still standing with my phone in my hand and Nicole screaming in the background when Firstborn jumped up.

"Mike, I know that you haven't forgot about the thirty kilos of coke on this gotdamn plane?"

"I'm aware of what's on board, Firstborn. Pierre made damn sure of that, before we left the island!" Rhynyia then looked at me yelling.

"Michael, you didn't?" She asked as she looked like I had just shitted on her heart.

"No, I didn't, Rhynyia! I told you before, that I don't get down like that." I then pointed over at my rock headed brother. "He did!"

She then looked over at him, then saying. "You do realize that you have made the biggest mistake in your young ass life, right?" Just as the last word had slipped off of her lips, she began slipping on some black attire, with me looking over at him, saying. "The girls are in trouble, and we have to get to them before it's too late!" We still hadn't been talking, so I didn't know what his response would be, until he opened up his mouth and said,

"Say less, my nigga! Once again it's on! Let's do what we do best, baby boy!" I couldn't do nothing but smile at my wild and crazy ass brother. Even though we were at odds, how could I not still love my nigga? We hugged one another, then I got back to Nicole. "I can trace them by their tracking devices on their phone, we're on the way!"

"But Mike, I thought that you all were in Puerto Rico?" She asked in a panic. "We were, but we're now on the plane in the air, headed to Jacksonville as we speak!" Then in her sexy ass voice she spoke back with,

"Hurry Mike, please! I'm going to try and wait at the club until you guys land," She said just as the call dropped.

"Damn!"

"What?" Rhynyia asked. "The call dropped." I then looked back over to Rhynyia and asked her. "Are there any weapons on board?" She was still changing when she pointed up over my head.

"Open the compartment up above your head, your weapon is inside there, along with one for Joe Rock Head!" He quickly turned to look at me, then Rhynyia.

"I heard that," he said as he held his hand out for his weapon. Just as he had received it, is when Maria came running back into the plane with, "Excuse me, Princess?"

"Yes Maria, what is it?"

"Miguel is having problems with Jacksonville International," she recited with beads of sweat dripping off of her forehead. "What?"

"I don't know, Senorita." Rhynyia looked over at me.

"Michael, come with me." She then reached out for my hand, leading me into the cockpit of the plane. Ten seconds later, her and I were standing inside the cockpit with Miguel, who had a disgusted look on his face.

"Senorita, we have the cocainia on the plane and they want to know the emergency of us landing there." He spoke with broken language. "I see, hold on, let me think this thing out for a minute." She spoke as she took a seat in the co-pilot's chair. Moments later, the answer seemed to have just fell in her lap. "Patch me through," she said to Miguel as she stared him directly in his eyes. In her lovely eyes, she showed no sign of fear at all.

"Yes Senorita."

I was just standing there, watching in disbelief when she said into the control device. "Jacksonville International! This is Princess Rhynyia Santiago from the island of Visgues. My father is Pierre Santiago. His private jet plane number is 1256. We have a medical emergency on board. We are requesting an emergency landing. Over!"

"Flight 1256, this is Jacksonville Tower, what is the emergency, over?" This is when she looked back at me, still standing there with a look of doubt on my face. She showed me her half smile as she came back with, "My fiancé has symptoms of a Flu-like virus and it seems as if he's having a seizure of some sort! We need to land immediately, over!" There was a brief pause in the communication as she turned to me still holding onto that smile.

"Flu-like symptoms, huh?" I asked as I smiled back at her.

"Flight 1256, we're sorry to hear that. You have clearance for an emergency landing. After landing, hangar 22 will be made available for you and your crew. Princess, over."

Her half smile then turned into a full one as she replied, "Thank you tower, have an ambulance waiting so we can get him to the hospital, please, over."

"Flight 1256, there is one in route, over."

"Thank you very much tower, over."

"No problem Princess, have a safe landing and we're glad to be of some assistance, over."

"Thank you tower, over." She then stood up, kissing me on the cheek, then looking down at Miguel. "You heard the man, now how long before we land?"

"Twenty minutes, Senorita," he stated, not even turning to look at her. He couldn't, his eyes were trained in on the instruments in front of him …

Rhynyia and I had just emerged back where the others were seated, when she shouted out. "Twenty minutes to landing, Natasha, you know what to do!" Her sister looked at her and then nodded her head up and down as she lazily walked over to what looked like a sound system. She then turned to Firstborn and I, holding a wicked smirk on her face. "Please listen to this song very carefully!" She then started placing on black attire as well as her sister. Then in our background, Phil Collins, In the Air Tonight, came through the high powered sound system. Just as she had tied up her hair in a black bandana, her and Rhynyia started singing along with the song. While my brother and I just sat there looking at them with a puzzled look on our faces. The drum portion of the classic hit song blasted through the system as Rhynyia jumped to her feet, holding up her Beretta 9mm with the laser red sighting. She would tell me later, that the song was a true song about a guy drowning, while another guy just sat there and did nothing. Phil Collins was there when this was taking place and couldn't get to the guy, but the other guy could. Well the guy that was drowning died that night. Years later, the guy that could have helped him, showed up at one of Phil' shows. Phil remembered his face as the guy walked up to him smiling, trying to shake his hand, but Phil slapped his hand away, due to him remembering that the guy was the guy who didn't save the guy…

The song was still playing as she looked to me and said. "This is what we do, Michael!" I just sat there still gazing at her as if she was crazy and had lost her rabbit ass mind.

"What kind of daughters had Pierre Santiago muthafucking raise?" I asked myself as I felt the plane make a slight adjustment in its flight pattern, headed straight for Jacksonville International.

"Alright, turn it down for a minute, Tasha."

"Okay," her sister said as she stood up to turn down the volume. "Alright everyone, listen closely for just a moment. I've bought us some time at the airport, before anyone gets suspicious about the plane."

"What do you mean?" I asked as I sat there dumb founded.

"Michael, are you for real?" Rhynyia asked as she looked at me with a dumb ass look on her face.

"Yes, for real."

"My father's drugs are on this plane and if we we're to get caught with them on here, there's a good fucking chance that we might not never see daylight again!" She said as she looked directly at my black ass.

"She's right bro." My brother agreed as I looked back at his ass and said.

"Seriously? It's your damn fault why there on this fucking plane, block headed ass nigga!

"Mike, please calm down, there's no time for that now. So just listen."

"My bad," I uttered.

"Yeah, lil ass nigga! Sit your ass down before I knock your ass down!" I stared hard at my brother before I replied. "Whatever, when this shit is over nigga, it's gone be me and you!" I had fire in my eyes as I sat back down, heart pounding a mile a minute.

"Guys, for real? My fucking sisters are in trouble and you two want to fight? Now!"

"Sorry, Rhynyia," I said as she then said. "Okay, so here's the plan. Once we land and pull to the hanger, there should be an ambulance there waiting for us. Michael, you're going to pretend to be sick, once we get you inside the ambulance, we're going to have to hijack the ambulance so that we can get to where the girls are."

"What?"

"The ambulance, Michael. That's our only way to getting to where they are."

"But what about the people driving the ambulance, how sure are you that we can trust them?"

"You're right Michael, that's why we're going to knock them out or somehow convince them to go along with the plan...

Chapter 35
Wow!

I stood up, placing my hands up in the air, then saying. "I don't know about that one guys. How in the hell are we supposed to just take over a goddamn ambulance, with attendants on the bitch?"

Then Firstborn said one of the brightest things that his dumb ass had ever said before. "Mike, hold on. I think I got it!"

"What?"

"Listen, the money from the cops."

"Okay, what about it?"

"We just hand over a few stacks and then go from there."

Rhynyia then stood up, while looking over at him, then me. "You know, he might just be onto something here, Michael." She paused. "It's worth a try."

"Yeah whatever. I guess, what other choice do we have?" I asked as the fasten your seat belt sign came back on. "We can always just kill them and rid of the entire situation," Natasha chimed in. We all stared at her, sitting there with a crazy ass unit on her face.

"Her ass is dead ass serious, Mike."

Rhynyia stated, "I know, but hell no! There has been too much killing already. Let's just stick with my brother's plan, okay. Now that that is over, here we go." I mouthed as I sat back down...

The twin engine private luxury jet plane landed in Jacksonville twenty minutes later, just like Miguel had said. As soon as he slowed the plane down, we were taxied over to hangar 22, where the ambulance and attendants were waiting for us. Just as soon as the door of the plane opened up, Rhynyia and her sister were met at the bottom of the stairs by a young black driver.

"Princess Rhynyia, I presume?" He asked as he held out his hand for her.

"Yes. My fiancé is upstairs. Where's the gurney?" She asked as she smiled at the young black driver, he couldn't be no older than twenty five. He blushed when Rhynyia smiled at his young ass.

"Right here, ma'am." The nurse said as she hurried from the back of the ambulance. The gurney was then brought on board as I pretended to be sick, but once they saw me and my condition, the gig was up.

Ten long minutes of Rhynyia and I telling the two what the deal was and not to mention the thirty bands a piece that was handed to them, they gave into what we had planned. Five minutes later, the ambulance was speeding out of Jacksonville International towards the Murder Queens destination. But right before we had left, my brother was back to where some of the cocaine was stored. He would tell me later, that he had to look at all the coke that Pierre had given to him, one more time, before we left. Talking about, he wanted to make sure he remembered it just like it was, because he didn't trust the people on the plane with it when we left. Truth be told, the over jealous brother just couldn't believe that the man had trusted him with that much product.

Rhynyia and her sister were sitting across from me and my brother, with the two paid attendants up front, driving. "Their destination is only ten minutes away from here!" I said as I looked up at Rhynyia from my phone's tracking app.

"Cool. Don't you think that you should tell the driver the address?" she said as she broke out into a smile.

"Yeah, hold on." I then alerted the driver of the address. Then sitting back down next to my brother. Who was trying to ask Rhynyia a question.

"Excuse me, Rhynyia?" He asked.

"Yes."

"Why don't you want me to go into business with your father?" She then held her head down, smile gone from her face. She then began to shake her head from side to side, then looking back up at him and I.

"What did my father say to you if you fucked up his money and precious product."

"He never did. Why?" She then looked over to me. This is where in the story, that my entire world would be rocked, by what she answered me with.

"Michael, did he say anything to you about fucking up his money or product?" I duly looked back at her with a dejected facial expression. My brother was staring at me also, eyes wide as fuck.

"Yes. He said that if my brother fucked up his money and product, that he would send some people called, THEM to find us. Me and my immediate family members."

She then placed her head back down and before she could even say another word, her sister pulled out a tech nine and chambered the automatic weapon, then she pointed it at my brother and spoke.

"He was referring to us, Firstborn. My sisters and I are who he calls, THEM! The ones that have to go out and take care of the ones who fuck over our father's money and precious product!" She had fucked up my entire mental with that. As him and I sat there with our mouths wide the fuck open, she finished with,

"That's why we're so highly trained with weapons. My sister and I handle the weapons part of this highly elite trained team of dangerous ladies, while our sister Countess handles the chemical portion.

"Damn! So, what does the little one do?" I asked as I sat there, still shaking my head in sheer disbelief.

"The little one is very dangerous." There was another brief pause. Then Rhynyia looked at me and said, "That little heifer handles all of the explosives!" This is when I acted as if I couldn't believe what my ears were hearing.

"Explosives?"

"Yes, explosives!"

"Damn! That's some serious ass shit," Firstborn remarked, as all I could do was utter. "Wow!"

I was seated there stunned after mentally trying to process what I had just heard coming from the lips of her and her sister. Her damn sister hadn't even muttered two words the entire time that we were over in Puerto Rico, on that goddamn small ass island that Rhynyia asked me to never tell anyone about.

After they had given us the spill about her and her sisters. Natasha quietly whispered. "My code name is Black Widow."

"Black Widow!" My dumb ass brother asked as one lone tear decided to snake down the right side of his round ass face.

"Yes, Black Widow." She spoke back, proudly.

"What in God's name have I done?" He stuttered as he placed his face in the palm of his open hands, while bending over, slightly sobbing. Rhynyia and her sister then placed their hands on his shoulder, while his head hung low. And then said in unison.

"Frankly, you have signed the death certificates for you and your precious baby brother, if you are to ever fuck over our father's money and product!" Rhynyia then looked over to me, before saying, "Now hold your head up and become the man that I know you are!" As he brought his head up, loutishly, you could hear him sniffling as if he was trying to keep us from knowing that he was crying. Just as his head had come up, he cut his eyes over at me, with me having a single tear in my left eye.

"Thanks bro," I muttered. Then hit his ass with, "So this is what it's all about, Manny?"

He turned his head slightly over in my direction, then telling me with his mouth turned sideways. "Manny, nigga my fucking name isn't no damn Manny!"

"I know that, ole silly ass boy! It's what Scarface said to his partner when they were out at dinner, right before shit started hitting the fan!" He then blew out some hot air, before uttering.

"Man, I don't want to die!"

"I know, right. Neither do I. So if you have to kill me, you would kill me, Rhynyia?" I asked her as she looked at me and said.

"Michael, please don't make me have to choose between you and my father."

Her sister then looked at my brother and recited. "Yeah and don't make me have to kill you, since I have mad feelings for your ass!" He just sat there looking like he had just fucked the devil.

After all of that had took place, I realized that I still had to call Nicole back. So I dialed her number once again. This time, nervous as hell.

"Who are you calling now?" Rhynyia asked me.

"Nicole, I need to find out has she heard from Mignon and the girls yet?"

Nicole answered on the second ring, sounding like she was whispering. "Hello, Mike, where are you guys?"

"Two minutes away Nicole, why, where are you?"

"I'm already here at that warehouse. And it looks like them niggas have the girls inside without any of their clothes on," she said to me as my head dropped.

"What?" I asked, not wanting to know. But fear was choking the shit out of my ass as I waited for her to reply. "The girls are all naked and some of the guys inside are naked too. By the looks of things there about to rape them first, then kill each and every one of them." Tears of anger and built up rage consumed my eyes as the ambulance bent a curve trying to get there before the ladies met their awful fate. Then Nicole said something to me that froze my heart,

"Mike, I have to go ... but know that I will always love you, no matter what." Was the last words that I heard, before I heard someone's gun go ... *Blak-blak!*

"Nicole, Nicole!" I screamed as the ambulance swerved to one side of the road, before the other attendant reached out for the steering wheel and guided the ambulance back on its course, all due to the damn driver trying to pull on a fucking blunt that he was trying to smoke.

"Fuck! What in the hell are you two doing up there?" Rhynyia yelled.

"My bad." The driver screamed.

"Remind me to kill that brother when this shit is all over with!" Natasha said as she regained her composure.

"Girl, chill," Rhynyia said as she looked over at her sister. Seconds later, we all had pulled up to the abandoned warehouse. A few minutes 2 fucking late ...

To be continued ...

Lock Down Publications and Ca$h Presents
Assisted Publishing Packages

BASIC PACKAGE	UPGRADED PACKAGE
$499	$800
Editing	Typing
Cover Design	Editing
Formatting	Cover Design
	Formatting
ADVANCE PACKAGE	**LDP SUPREME PACKAGE**
$1,200	$1,500
Typing	Typing
Editing	Editing
Cover Design	Cover Design
Formatting	Formatting
Copyright registration	Copyright registration
Proofreading	Proofreading
Upload book to Amazon	Set up Amazon account
	Upload book to Amazon
	Advertise on LDP, Amazon and Facebook Page

***Other services available upon request.
Additional charges may apply

Lock Down Publications
P.O. Box 944
Stockbridge, GA 30281-9998
Phone: 470 303-9761

Submission Guideline

Submit the first three chapters of your completed manuscript to ldpsubmissions@gmail.com. In the subject line add **Your Book's Title**. The manuscript must be in a Word Doc file and sent as an attachment. Document should be in Times New Roman, double spaced, and in size 12 font. Also, provide your synopsis and full contact information. If sending multiple submissions, they must each be in a separate email.

Have a story but no way to send it electronically? You can still submit to LDP/Ca$h Presents. Send in the first three chapters, written or typed, of your completed manuscript to:

LDP: Submissions Dept
P.O. Box 944
Stockbridge, GA 30281-9998

DO NOT send original manuscript. Must be a duplicate.
Provide your synopsis and a cover letter containing your full contact information.

Thanks for considering LDP and Ca$h Presents.

NEW RELEASES

BLOODLINE OF A SAVAGE 1&2
THESE VICIOUS STREETS
RELENTLESS GOON
RELENTLESS GOON 2
BY PRINCE A. TAUHID

THE BUTTERFLY MAFIA 1-3
BY FUMIYA PAYNE

A THUG'S STREET PRINCESS 1&2
BY MEESHA

CITY OF SMOKE 2
BY MOLOTTI

STEPPERS 1,2&3
BY KING RIO

THE LANE 1&2
BY KEN-KEN SPENCE

THUG OF SPADES 1&2
LOVE IN THE TRENCHES 2
BY COREY ROBINSON

TIL DEATH 3
BY ARYANNA

THE BIRTH OF A GANGSTER 4
BY DELMONT PLAYER

PRODUCT OF THE STREETS 1&2
BY DEMOND "MONEY" ANDERSON

NO TIME FOR ERROR
BY KEESE

MONEY HUNGRY DEMONS
BY TRANAY ADAMS

Coming Soon from Lock Down Publications/Ca$h Presents

IF YOU CROSS ME ONCE 6
ANGEL V
By Anthony Fields

IMMA DIE BOUT MINE 4&5
By Aryanna

A THUGS STREET PRINCESS 3
By Meesha

PRODUCT OF THE STREETS 3
By Demond Money Anderson

CORNER BOYS
By Corey Robinson

SON OF A DOPE FIEND 4
By Renta

THE MURDER QUEENS 6&7
By Michael Gallon

CITY OF SMOKE 3
By Molotti

BETRAYAL OF A G
By Ray Vinci

CONFESSIONS OF A DOPE BOY
By Nicholas Lock

THA TAKEOVER
By Keith Chandler

Available Now

RESTRAINING ORDER 1 & 2
By **CA$H & Coffee**

LOVE KNOWS NO BOUNDARIES 1-3
By **Coffee**

RAISED AS A GOON I, II, III & IV
BRED BY THE SLUMS I, II, III
BLAST FOR ME I & II
ROTTEN TO THE CORE I II III
A BRONX TALE I, II, III
DUFFLE BAG CARTEL I II III IV V VI
HEARTLESS GOON I II III IV V
A SAVAGE DOPEBOY I II
DRUG LORDS I II III
CUTTHROAT MAFIA I II
KING OF THE TRENCHES
By **Ghost**

LAY IT DOWN I & II
LAST OF A DYING BREED I II
BLOOD STAINS OF A SHOTTA I & II III
By **Jamaica**

LOYAL TO THE GAME I II III
LIFE OF SIN I, II III
By **TJ & Jelissa**

IF LOVING HIM IS WRONG...I & II
LOVE ME EVEN WHEN IT HURTS I II III
By **Jelissa**

BLOODY COMMAS I & II
SKI MASK CARTEL I, II & III
KING OF NEW YORK I II, III IV V
RISE TO POWER I II III
COKE KINGS I II III IV V
BORN HEARTLESS I II III IV
KING OF THE TRAP I II
By **T.J. Edwards**

WHEN THE STREETS CLAP BACK I & II III
THE HEART OF A SAVAGE I II III IV
MONEY MAFIA I II
LOYAL TO THE SOIL I II III
By **Jibril Williams**

A DISTINGUISHED THUG STOLE MY HEART I II &
III
LOVE SHOULDN'T HURT I II III IV
RENEGADE BOYS 1-4
PAID IN KARMA 1-3
SAVAGE STORMS 1-3
AN UNFORESEEN LOVE 1-3
BABY, I'M WINTERTIME COLD 1-3
A THUG'S STREET PRINCESS 1&2
By **Meesha**

A GANGSTER'S CODE 1-3
A GANGSTER'S SYN 1-3
THE SAVAGE LIFE 1-3
CHAINED TO THE STREETS 1-3
BLOOD ON THE MONEY 1-3
A GANGSTA'S PAIN 1-3
BEAUTIFUL LIES AND UGLY TRUTHS
CHURCH IN THESE STREETS
By **J-Blunt**

PUSH IT TO THE LIMIT
By **Bre' Hayes**

BLOOD OF A BOSS 1-5
SHADOWS OF THE GAME
TRAP BASTARD
By **Askari**

THE STREETS BLEED MURDER 1-3
THE HEART OF A GANGSTA 1-3
By **Jerry Jackson**

CUM FOR ME 1-8
An LDP Erotica Collaboration

BRIDE OF A HUSTLA 1-3
THE FETTI GIRLS 1-3
CORRUPTED BY A GANGSTA 1-4
BLINDED BY HIS LOVE
THE PRICE YOU PAY FOR LOVE 1-3
DOPE GIRL MAGIC 1-3
By **Destiny Skai**

WHEN A GOOD GIRL GOES BAD
By **Adrienne**

A KINGPIN'S AMBITION
A KINGPIN'S AMBITION II
I MURDER FOR THE DOUGH
By **Ambitious**

THE COST OF LOYALTY 1-3
By **Kweli**

A GANGSTER'S REVENGE 1-4
THE BOSS MAN'S DAUGHTERS 1-5
A SAVAGE LOVE 1&2
BAE BELONGS TO ME 1&2
A HUSTLER'S DECEIT 1-3
WHAT BAD BITCHES DO 1-3
SOUL OF A MONSTER 1-3
KILL ZONE
A DOPE BOY'S QUEEN 1-3
TIL DEATH 1-3
IMMA DIE BOUT MINE 1-3
By **Aryanna**

TRUE SAVAGE 1-7
DOPE BOY MAGIC 1-3
MIDNIGHT CARTEL 1-3
CITY OF KINGZ 1&2
NIGHTMARE ON SILENT AVE
THE PLUG OF LIL MEXICO 1&2
CLASSIC CITY
By **Chris Green**

A DOPEBOY'S PRAYER
By **Eddie "Wolf" Lee**

THE KING CARTEL 1-3
By **Frank Gresham**

THESE NIGGAS AIN'T LOYAL 1-3
By **Nikki Tee**

GANGSTA SHYT 1-3
By **CATO**

THE ULTIMATE BETRAYAL
By **Phoenix**

BOSS'N UP 1-3
By **Royal Nicole**

I LOVE YOU TO DEATH
By **Destiny J**

I RIDE FOR MY HITTA
I STILL RIDE FOR MY HITTA
By **Misty Holt**

LOVE & CHASIN' PAPER
By **Qay Crockett**

TO DIE IN VAIN
SINS OF A HUSTLA
By **ASAD**

BROOKLYN HUSTLAZ
By **Boogsy Morina**

BROOKLYN ON LOCK 1 & 2
By **Sonovia**

GANGSTA CITY
By **Teddy Duke**

A DRUG KING AND HIS DIAMOND 1-3
A DOPEMAN'S RICHES
HER MAN, MINE'S TOO 1&2
CASH MONEY HO'S
THE WIFEY I USED TO BE 1&2
PRETTY GIRLS DO NASTY THINGS
By **Nicole Goosby**

LIPSTICK KILLAH 1-3
CRIME OF PASSION 1-3
FRIEND OR FOE 1-3
By **Mimi**

TRAPHOUSE KING 1-3
KINGPIN KILLAZ 1-3
STREET KINGS 1&2
PAID IN BLOOD 1&2
CARTEL KILLAZ 1-3
DOPE GODS 1&2
By **Hood Rich**

STEADY MOBBN' 1-3
THE STREETS STAINED MY SOUL 1-3
By **Marcellus Allen**

WHO SHOT YA 1-3
SON OF A DOPE FIEND 1-3
HEAVEN GOT A GHETTO 1&2
SKI MASK MONEY 1&2
By **Renta**

GORILLAZ IN THE BAY 1-4
TEARS OF A GANGSTA 1/&2
3X KRAZY 1&2
STRAIGHT BEAST MODE 1&2
By **DE'KARI**

TRIGGADALE 1-3
MURDA WAS THE CASE 1-3
By **Elijah R. Freeman**

THE STREETS ARE CALLING
By **Duquie Wilson**

SLAUGHTER GANG 1-3
RUTHLESS HEART 1-3
By **Willie Slaughter**

GOD BLESS THE TRAPPERS 1-3
THESE SCANDALOUS STREETS 1-3
FEAR MY GANGSTA 1-5
THESE STREETS DON'T LOVE NOBODY 1-2
BURY ME A G 1-5
A GANGSTA'S EMPIRE 1-4
THE DOPEMAN'S BODYGAURD 1&2
THE REALEST KILLAZ 1-3
THE LAST OF THE OGS 1-3
By **Tranay Adams**

MARRIED TO A BOSS 1-3
By **Destiny Skai & Chris Green**

KINGZ OF THE GAME 1-7
CRIME BOSS 1-3
By **Playa Ray**

FUK SHYT
By **Blakk Diamond**

DON'T F#CK WITH MY HEART 1&2
By **Linnea**

ADDICTED TO THE DRAMA 1-3
IN THE ARM OF HIS BOSS
By **Jamila**

LOYALTY AIN'T PROMISED 1&2
By **Keith Williams**

YAYO 1-4
A SHOOTER'S AMBITION 1&2
BRED IN THE GAME
By **S. Allen**

TRAP GOD 1-3
RICH $AVAGE 1-3
MONEY IN THE GRAVE 1-3
CARTEL MONEY
By **Martell Troublesome Bolden**

FOREVER GANGSTA 1&2
GLOCKS ON SATIN SHEETS 1&2
By **Adrian Dulan**

TOE TAGZ 1-4
LEVELS TO THIS SHYT 1&2
IT'S JUST ME AND YOU
By **Ah'Million**

KINGPIN DREAMS 1-3
RAN OFF ON DA PLUG
By **Paper Boi Rari**

CONFESSIONS OF A GANGSTA 1-4
CONFESSIONS OF A JACKBOY 1-3
CONFESSIONS OF A HITMAN
By **Nicholas Lock**

I'M NOTHING WITHOUT HIS LOVE
SINS OF A THUG
TO THE THUG I LOVED BEFORE
A GANGSTA SAVED XMAS
IN A HUSTLER I TRUST
By **Monet Dragun**

QUIET MONEY 1-3
THUG LIFE 1-3
EXTENDED CLIP 1&2
A GANGSTA'S PARADISE
By **Trai'Quan**

CAUGHT UP IN THE LIFE 1-3
THE STREETS NEVER LET GO 1-3
By **Robert Baptiste**

NEW TO THE GAME 1-3
MONEY, MURDER & MEMORIES 1-3
By **Malik D. Rice**

CREAM 2-3
THE STREETS WILL TALK
By **Yolanda Moore**

LIFE OF A SAVAGE 1-4
A GANGSTA'S QUR'AN 1-4
MURDA SEASON 1-3
GANGLAND CARTEL 1-3
CHI'RAQ GANGSTAS 1-4
KILLERS ON ELM STREET 1-3
JACK BOYZ N DA BRONX 1-3
A DOPEBOY'S DREAM 1-3
JACK BOYS VS DOPE BOYS 1-3
COKE GIRLZ
COKE BOYS
SOSA GANG 1&2
BRONX SAVAGES
BODYMORE KINGPINS
BLOOD OF A GOON
By **Romell Tukes**

THE MURDER QUEENS 6 | MICHAEL GALLON

THE STREETS MADE ME 1-3
By **Larry D. Wright**

CONCRETE KILLA 1-3
VICIOUS LOYALTY 1-3
By **Kingpen**

THE ULTIMATE SACRIFICE 1-6
KHADIFI
IF YOU CROSS ME ONCE 1-3
ANGEL 1-4
IN THE BLINK OF AN EYE
By **Anthony Fields**

THE LIFE OF A HOOD STAR
By **Ca$h & Rashia Wilson**

THE STREETS WILL NEVER CLOSE 1-3
By **K'ajji**

NIGHTMARES OF A HUSTLA 1-3
By **King Dream**

HARD AND RUTHLESS 1&2
MOB TOWN 251
THE BILLIONAIRE BENTLEYS 1-3
REAL G'S MOVE IN SILENCE
By **Von Diesel**

GHOST MOB
By **Stilloan Robinson**

MOB TIES 1-6
SOUL OF A HUSTLER, HEART OF A KILLER 1-3
GORILLAZ IN THE TRENCHES
By **SayNoMore**

BODYMORE MURDERLAND 1-3
THE BIRTH OF A GANGSTER 1-4
By **Delmont Player**

FOR THE LOVE OF A BOSS 1&2
By **C. D. Blue**

KILLA KOUNTY 1-5
By **Khufu**

MOBBED UP 1-4
THE BRICK MAN 1-5
THE COCAINE PRINCESS 1-10
STEPPERS 1-3
SUPER GREMLIN 1-4
By **King Rio**

MONEY GAME 1&2
By **Smoove Dolla**

A GANGSTA'S KARMA 1-4
By **FLAME**

KING OF THE TRENCHES 1-3
By **GHOST & TRANAY ADAMS**

QUEEN OF THE ZOO 1&2
By **Black Migo**

GRIMEY WAYS 1-3
By **Ray Vinci**

XMAS WITH AN ATL SHOOTER
By **Ca$h & Destiny Skai**

THE MURDER QUEENS 6 | MICHAEL GALLON

KING KILLA 1&2
By **Vincent "Vitto" Holloway**

BETRAYAL OF A THUG 1&2
By **Fre$h**

THE MURDER QUEENS 1-5
By **Michael Gallon**

FOR THE LOVE OF BLOOD 1-4
By **Jamel Mitchell**

HOOD CONSIGLIERE 1&2
NO TIME FOR ERROR
By **Keese**

PROTÉGÉ OF A LEGEND 1&2
LOVE IN THE TRENCHES 1&2
By **Corey Robinson**

BORN IN THE GRAVE 1-3
CRIME PAYS
By **Self Made Tay**

MOAN IN MY MOUTH
By **XTASY**

TORN BETWEEN A GANGSTER AND A GENTLEMAN
By **J-BLUNT & Miss Kim**

LOYALTY IS EVERYTHING 1-3
CITY OF SMOKE 1&2
By **Molotti**

HERE TODAY GONE TOMORROW 1&2
By **Fly Rock**

WOMEN LIE MEN LIE 1-4
FIFTY SHADES OF SNOW 1-3
STACK BEFORE YOU SPLURGE
GIRLS FALL LIKE DOMINOES
NAÏVE TO THE STREETS
By **ROY MILLIGAN**

PILLOW PRINCESS
By **S. Hawkins**

THE BUTTERFLY MAFIA 1-3
SALUTE MY SAVAGERY 1&2
By **Fumiya Payne**

THE LANE 1&2
By Ken-Ken Spence

THE PUSSY TRAP 1-5
By **Nene Capri**

DIRTY DNA
By **Blaque**

SANCTIFIED AND HORNY
by **XTASY**

BOOKS BY LDP'S CEO, CA$H

TRUST IN NO MAN
TRUST IN NO MAN 2
TRUST IN NO MAN 3
BONDED BY BLOOD
SHORTY GOT A THUG
THUGS CRY
THUGS CRY 2
THUGS CRY 3
TRUST NO BITCH
TRUST NO BITCH 2
TRUST NO BITCH 3
TIL MY CASKET DROPS
RESTRAINING ORDER
RESTRAINING ORDER 2
IN LOVE WITH A CONVICT
LIFE OF A HOOD STAR
XMAS WITH AN ATL SHOOTER